DEATH
OF A GHOST

The Hamish Macbeth series

DEATH
OF A GHOST

A Hamish Macbeth Murder Mystery

M.C. BEATON

Constable • London

CONSTABLE

First published in the United States by Grand Central Publishing,
a division of Hachette Book Group USA Inc., 2017

This edition published in Great Britain in 2017 by Constable

1 3 5 7 9 10 8 6 4 2

A CIP catalogue record for this book
is available from the British Library.

ISBN: 978-1-47211-724-3

Typeset in Palatino by Photoprint, Torquay
Printed and bound in Great Britain by
CPI Group (UK) Ltd, Croydon CR0 4YY

Papers used by Constable are from well-managed forests and other
responsible sources.

For my two angels,
Krystyna Green and David Shelley

Chapter One

The murmur of the ...
—Sydney ...

Police Sergeant Hamish ...

Chapter One

The murmur of the mourning ghost
—Sydney Thompson Dobell

Police Sergeant Hamish Macbeth was feeling trapped. He had started an affair with the head of the Strathbane forensic department, Christine Dalray, and had begun to feel as if he had been arrested. His police station home in the village of Lochdubh in Sutherland was no longer a refuge. He often thought wearily that he should have known that a woman who could head and command a department of boozy male chauvinists would be a control freak.

Christine was attractive to look at, with long legs and curly hair. But she managed his meals, his dress, and how they performed in bed. Hamish was afraid to ditch her in case she told the authorities that his sidekick, Police Constable Charlie Carter, was staying at a basement flat in the Tommel Castle Hotel. Charlie was too clumsy to have in the police station, but he was kind, hardworking, and amiable, which is why Hamish found himself one morning whistling for his dogs and fleeing

1

the station to join Charlie for breakfast before Christine woke.

So far, he had kept his worries about life with Christine to himself, but as he relaxed in Charlie's cosy little flat in front of the peat fire while Charlie fried sausages, he was overcome with a desire to share his troubles. So when breakfast was over, Hamish said awkwardly, 'I want rid of Christine.'

Charlie was a giant of a man, with child-like blue eyes and fair hair. 'I saw that coming,' he said. 'They call her Attila the Hun over at the lab, except the *H* in *Hun* is replaced with a *C* and the *T*—'

'I get the picture,' said Hamish hurriedly. 'Why didn't you tell me?'

'I thought you were all set for the altar,' said Charlie. 'What are you going to do?'

'I don't know. Think of something!'

'Have you asked the fairies?'

'For the umpteenth time, Charlie, there are no such things.'

Charlie sat with his head bowed. Now I know what *away with the fairies* really means, thought Hamish bitterly.

But Charlie suddenly looked up and grinned. 'I've got it!'

'Out with it.'

'Blair hates your guts, right?' Detective Chief Inspector Blair was the bane of Hamish's life.

'What's that got to do with anything?' asked Hamish.

2

'It's like this. I'll go down to Strathbane and gossip about how you are so mad about Christine that if she left you it would break your heart. Blair would move mountains to bring that about.'

'Och,' said Hamish, 'he'll tell her awful things about me and as she knows how much the scunner hates me, she won't listen.'

'He's not that daft. Worth a try.'

Perhaps the fairies had taken against Hamish Macbeth because Charlie's plan worked in the worst way possible. Two days later, he was summoned to police headquarters to face Superintendent Daviot.

Daviot was in a foul mood. Eight Scottish police departments had been merged into one called Police Scotland, which seemed to mean it had become a sort of state within a state with enough form-filling, paperwork, and bureaucracy to make a French bureaucrat weep with envy. He gazed over the pile of paperwork on his desk as Hamish was ushered in.

'Sit down,' he said. 'It's time we had a man-to-man talk.'

Hamish sat down and put his cap at his feet. Daviot was a grey man: grey hair, grey eyes, and grey suit. He considered Macbeth a maverick. Surely his flaming-red hair couldn't be natural.

'It has come to my ears,' said Daviot, 'that you are cohabiting with a member of the force.'

'I am not having an affair with a policewoman,' said Hamish.

'No, but the forensic department is part of Police Scotland and there are people always on the lookout for some . . . well, let us call it breaches of police etiquette.'

'You are quite right, sir,' said Hamish meekly. 'I shall end the affair today.'

Daviot suddenly smiled indulgently, remembering that any breakup would upset Hamish dreadfully.

'Now, now, Hamish. Just marry the lady and I will be your best man. There! Never say we are hardhearted.'

Stunned, Hamish thanked him and walked from the room. Daviot's secretary, Helen, who had been listening at the door, smiled maliciously. 'He'll make a decent man of you yet,' she jeered.

The suddenly vague look in Hamish's eyes should have warned her that the policeman was thinking of some nasty way he could get back at her. Then he pushed open the superintendent's door and went back in.

'Sir,' said Hamish, 'I could not help noticing you have a great deal of paperwork. Can't you delegate some of it?'

'No. A lot of these are marked "For Your Eyes Only".'

'But your trusted secretary is in fact your eyes, sir, and she has dealt with all the paperwork in the past and so would know better than any of us what to do.'

Daviot beamed. 'I am most grateful to you, and Helen will be honoured. Don't forget to send me a wedding invitation.'

Helen backed away from the door as Hamish came out. She opened her mouth to speak but the buzzer on Daviot's desk summoned her. Hamish went off, whistling, until he realized he would now have to cope with Christine.

He drove slowly back to Lochdubh. He stopped on the road and let his two dogs, Sally, a poodle, and Lugs, a mixed breed with odd blue eyes, out to play in the heather. He missed his wild cat that he had let loose in the wild cat sanctuary at Ardnamurchan. He was just whistling to them to get back in the Land Rover when he saw Christine's car speeding up the road towards where he was parked. She screeched to a halt and got out.

'So you're just another of these bastards who thinks that women belong in the kitchen,' she raged. 'Daviot informs me that once we are married, I have to quit my job. He told me it was all your idea. So, get this. I have phoned Glasgow and they're glad to have me back. Keep out of my way, you bastard, until I get my stuff packed and out of this peasant-hole of a dump.'

Hamish opened his mouth to protest but a sudden vision of having his station back all to himself rose in his brain and he said, 'But you'd make the grand wee wifie.'

He then stood with his head bowed as she let loose a raging tirade, ending up telling him he could take his male chauvinist ideas and shove them up his scrawny arse.

He decided to go to the pub in Lochdubh to allow time for Christine to get clear.

5

When he walked into the pub, four forestry workers hurried out, frightened that Hamish would take away their car keys. Hamish saw Archie Maclean seated at a table by the window, ordered a double tonic water, and went to join the fisherman.

'I hear she's leaving you,' said Archie.

'It's a right gossipy place,' said Hamish sourly, 'except when I'm trying to solve a crime. Then everyone's seen nothing, don't know nothing.'

'It's the idleness,' said Archie sententiously. 'See, at the moment, there arenae the tourist folk.' Archie augmented his fishing with taking tourists round the loch in the summer. 'Now, right now I'm hiding out from the wifie. Women get ower-bossy, Hamish, when they think you might be enjoying a bit of a lazy time.'

'You mean I need a murder?'

'That would have helped.'

'I don't like bullies,' said Hamish. 'And talking of bullies, when are you going to tell that wife of yours to stop boiling your clothes? I mean, whoever heard of a woman boiling tweed. That jacket of yours would fit a bairn. You stood up to her once.'

Hamish heard a voice from outside calling, 'Has anyone seen Archie?'

Archie darted across the pub and crouched down behind the bar. Mrs Maclean came in, eyes darting to right and left. She was a short, thin woman who smelled of bleach.

'Have you see Archie?' she demanded, stopping by Hamish's table.

6

'Saw him outside,' said Hamish. 'The poor wee man was off to the doctor.'

'What's up wi' him?'

'He's got strangulitis.'

'Whit's that?'

'It's a soreness in the balls caused by constriction.'

She let out a squawk of dismay and hurried off. Hamish went to the bar and leaned over. 'Get yourself to Dr Brodie and I'll warn him. Out the back way and with any luck you'll get there before her.'

Archie said, 'She'll have gone hame for her best bonnet.'

Hamish returned to his table and phoned the doctor and explained Archie's soon-to-arrive visit. 'He's got to get into comfortable clothes or his arteries will close up wi' the constriction,' said Hamish.

'I'll do my best,' said Dr Brodie, sounding amused.

'How did you get the news so quickly?' he called after Archie.

'Herself was in Patel's buying fags and she told the whole shop. She called you—'

'Okay, Archie. I'd rather imagine it. I think it's damn odd that she smokes, her and her tofu and salads.'

'I think maybe you should get along there. Mr Patel has a cheap line in red paint and she bought a can.'

'I don't care,' said Hamish uneasily. 'I am not having another confrontation.'

'When you get back, I'd throw out all your food,' said

7

Archie. 'I saw this documentary and there are all these wee sneaky poisons.'

'What I need,' said Hamish, 'is a nice crime.'

'Aye. Well, you may be having it. I've just seen Charlie walk past the window. I'd best be off before the wife gets to the surgery.'

The door opened and Charlie walked in, banged his head on a beam, tripped over a chair, and landed all of his over-six-foot length on the pub floor.

He got to his feet, rubbed his blonde hair, and looked sheepishly at Hamish.

'We've got an odd report from Drim,' said Charlie.

'Sit down and join us,' said Hamish. 'You're looming.'

Charlie sat down and winced as the chair gave a sinister creaking sound. 'It's a ghost,' he said.

'So who's the potty one ower in Drim who thinks they've seen a ghost? Saturday night when the pubs scale, I get reports of ghosts and fairies and things that go bump in the night.'

'Aye, but this is from Hanover Ebrington at the castle.'

'Is that the new owner? But the place is half a ruin.'

'He's a retired police superintendent from Glasgow so we'd better jump to it,' said Charlie.

'Oh, michty. The man's probably a drunk. Let's go.'

There are many castles in the Highlands, a lot of them mere ruins. Castle Drim had once been habitable but it was up on a bluff overlooking Loch Drim and the gales of Sutherland had done a lot to destroy a part of it.

8

'He *must* be a drunk,' complained Hamish as they took the one-track road to Drim. 'The Highlands are crammed wi' folk who've sozzled their brains into romantic dreams of Bonnie Prince Charlie and all that.'

'Disnae matter,' said Charlie gloomily. 'He was a police super, right? So he'll throw his weight around. You shouldnae hae brought your dogs along.'

As they approached the castle, Hamish noticed scaffolding at the front. The short drive had recently been cleared of weeds, and gravel had been put down. He remembered that the eighteenth-century bit at the front was habitable but the fifteenth-century bit to the left of the main entrance was in ruins.

He wondered if his arch enemy, Detective Chief Inspector Blair, had already arrived.

He imagined the retired super would be pugnacious and rude like Blair. The door was opened by a grey-haired man with a pleasant weather-beaten face. He held out a hand in welcome. 'I am Hanover. Stupid name. I am usually called Handy. And you are ... ?'

'Sergeant Hamish Macbeth of Lochdubh, sir, and Constable Carter.'

'Come in and we'll have some coffee and I'll tell you all about it.'

They found themselves in a small square hall. Hamish remembered it as being vast.

'Yes, I divided the hall up,' said Handy, answering the unspoken question. 'We'll use my study.'

He opened a door and led them into a comfortable room. A coal fire was blazing. Two high-backed leather armchairs were on either side of the fire with a sofa and coffee table placed in front of the hearth. A flat-screen television was mounted on the wall. There were two landscapes of highland scenes. A tall bookcase filled up one wall, the bottom shelves full of leather-bound books and the upper shelves crammed with brightly covered paperbacks. A worn Persian carpet covered the floor. An old console table held an array of bottles.

Handy sat in one of the armchairs and Hamish sat opposite him. Charlie lowered himself carefully onto the sofa, a smile on his face as he realized he had managed to enter the room without breaking anything.

The door opened and a woman came in carrying a tray laden with coffee and biscuits. 'Help yourselves,' she said curtly and shuffled out on a pair of old carpet slippers.

'That's my sister, Freda,' said Handy. 'Sour-faced old besom. Who's going to be mother?'

'I'll pour,' said Hamish.

'Black for me,' said Handy.

Handy had a pleasant Glasgow accent. Because of Blair's harsh guttural tones, Hamish had forgotten there was such a thing. 'I suppose you think I've been drinking whisky,' he said, 'but it's really scary. It comes from the old ruined end of the place. I'll take you there when you've had your coffee. Always at night. It starts up just after midnight, moaning and groaning. Of course I've gone to investigate, but there's nothing there and the sound comes from all around. I can't get any of the folk up from the village. They say they're scared to death.'

'And it's always at night?' asked Hamish.

'Yes.'

'Charlie and I will bring our sleeping bags along this evening and we'll see if we can find out anything.'

'Maybe,' said Charlie, 'two people would frighten away the ghostie.'

Hamish realized his highly superstitious sidekick was beginning to believe in the existence of ghosts. Well, it was time he learned there just weren't any such things.

'As I said, we'll both be here tonight.'

'Right,' said Handy. 'I'll show you where it is.'

On the other side of the hall was a massive oak door. He unlocked it to reveal a large round room, probably the remains of a tower. A lot of Scottish castles are simply tall buildings of about six storeys, sometimes with a tower at one corner and crowstep gables. Only the tower bit remained, or what was left of it. The roof was open to the sky in places, and the wind howled through old arrow slits. Charlie clutched Hamish.

'Get off!' said Hamish. 'It's only the wind.'

'Aye, it was more than that, Hamish,' said Handy. 'Like screams from hell.'

Hamish felt a little jolt of pleasure at being on first-name terms with a chief superintendent even though the man was retired.

'We won't disturb you any more,' said Hamish. 'We'll be back at midnight.'

'Come before then and have a dram and something to eat, lads, say about eight.'

'Thank you,' said Hamish. He grinned. 'I think our Charlie will need a bit o' Dutch courage.'

'What is it, Mr Blair?' Chief Superintendent Daviot was demanding, just as Hamish and Charlie were climbing into the Land Rover.

'You know, sir,' said Blair, his pudgy hands folded and an oily expression on his groggy face, 'that we like to treat folk equal, rich and poor alike. I 'member a speech o' yours and—'

'Get to the point,' snapped Daviot.

'It's just that Macbeth has had a report from some new owner of Castle Drim that it's haunted. I heard a report that he and Carter had gone to investigate. There was this shoplifting ower at Cnothan but they werenae available.'

'This is disgraceful. Tell Macbeth to get over to Cnothan. I will tell this new owner personally that we cannot be wasting police time. What is his name?'

Blair sniggered and then said, 'Hanover Ebrington.'

'Bound to be some jumped-up southerner,' said Daviot, 'hoping to give himself a bit of class by buying a ruin. Ask Helen on your road out to get his phone number.'

Blair could not rouse Hamish and was made furious when a call came in that the shoplifting culprit had been discovered and it was only some 'poor old biddie' with dementia.

Meanwhile, Daviot, having secured the number, dialled it, looking forward to giving this upstart a putting-down.

'This is Chief Superintendent Daviot of the Strathbane police.'

'Do you still call it that?' asked Handy. 'I thought it was all Police Scotland now.'

'Never mind that,' snapped Daviot. 'I would have you know, Mr Ebrington, that my staff have more to do with their time than play at ghost busters.'

'Don't patronize me,' said Handy in a quiet voice, somehow more menacing than if he had shouted. 'I've had more years of experience and commendations than you've had hot dinners. Someone is deliberately frightening the people of the village and I want to find out who it is.'

'You were in the force yourself?' asked Daviot.

'Chief super. Retired as soon as Police stupid Scotland came along.'

'Mr Ebrington. I assure you, sir, the situation was badly described to me. Is Macbeth looking into it?'

'Yes, he is. Courteous chap. You lot could learn from him.'

The phone was slammed down.

Daviot pressed the button on his desk. 'Helen,' he said, 'I am in need of a Tunnock's tea cake, and send Blair to me.'

* * *

'Let's go down to the village,' said Hamish. 'I remember when there was a murder here and then the minister's wife made a film. A lot of tourists came. Just want to make sure they're not trying to drum up trade.'

It was a windy spring day with great clouds sending shadows racing across the loch and surrounding mountains. The village lay at the end of a long sea loch on a flat piece of land. The loch was black as it was a thin sort of corridor between the walls of the mountains on either side: black mountains nearly devoid of any softening greenery at all, where little grew among the rock and scree but stunted bushes. The village of Drim consisted of a huddle of houses with the general store at one end and the church at the other, a round church, because everyone knew that evil spirits could only live in corners.

'There's a new minister here,' said Hamish. 'Let's call on him first.'

'Didn't think the kirk could afford to put a minister in this wee place,' said Charlie.

'It's a good manse, and the poor soul is expected to preach at four other villages on the Sabbath.'

'Haven't you called on him afore this?' asked Charlie curiously. 'You aye call on newcomers.'

'Not all,' said Hamish. 'They've been three of them afore this one. I'm surprised he lasted the winter.'

'What's his name?'

'Peter Haggis.'

'I'll bet he gets teased about his name.'

14

'You forget, Charlie. Ministers are treated with respect. He's not married.'

Hamish rang the brass bell set into the sandstone wall of the manse beside the door.

The door was opened by a thin, angry-looking woman. Hamish guessed her to be in her forties. She had dusty-black hair pulled up into a knot on the top of her head. Her sallow face had deep lines on either side of her full-lipped mouth. Her eyes were large and quite beautiful, brown with flecks of gold, like a peat stream with the sunlight glinting on it.

Hamish introduced them, explained the reason for his call, and asked to see the minister.

'I don't think that would be a good idea,' she said.

'Why is that and who are you?' demanded Hamish.

'I'm his sister, Sheila.'

'Sheila!' The minister appeared behind his sister. 'Why must you always leave people standing on the step? Come ben, gentlemen. How can I assist you?'

He was a small man with thick grey hair, a sensuous mouth, and small blue eyes.

Hamish and Charlie, with their caps tucked under their arms, followed him into what was obviously his study. It was lined with ancient dusty tomes. Hamish suddenly remembered being in this room before and the books looked the same, the historical leavings of previous ministers, no doubt stretching back to John Knox. Were they printing books in the time of Mary, Queen of Scots?

15

The Reverend Peter Haggis stared impatiently at the tall policeman with the flaming-red hair, who was standing with his mouth a little open, his hazel eyes vague.

'Why are you here?' demanded Peter sharply.

'It is about the haunting at Drim castle,' said Charlie.

'Oh, forget that,' said Peter briskly. 'Nothing but the wind. Take my advice and leave well alone. The locals are too superstitious as it is. Oh, what now, Sheila?' His sister was just backing into the room, holding a tray laden with coffee cups, a coffeepot, and biscuits. 'No, they're leaving,' he shouted. 'Take that muck away!'

Hamish and Charlie followed Sheila out into the small dark hall. 'You brother is very frightened,' said Hamish.

She swung the front door open. 'Sod off!' she yelled. 'And don't come back!'

Hamish's mobile phone rang. 'It's Daviot,' he muttered. 'Yes, sir?'

'You are to give all your time to finding out where these ghostly noises are coming from. Do I make myself clear?'

'I haven't stopped working on it,' said Hamish, puzzled.

'Good, good. Keep at it.'

'Has everyone gone daft?' said Hamish, after he had told Charlie about Daviot's call.

'I waud think that our friend Blair found out and told Daviot you were wasting police time. Daviot then finds out about Handy having been a chief superintendent and starts to grovel. And talking about daft, some o' the cottages have crossed rowan branches on the door.'

16

'Could be play-acting. Let's try the shop and see what Jock Kennedy has to say about all this. If you get the dogs out, I'll get us a couple of mutton pies and beer. Jock does the best mutton pies in Scotland, and my pampered pets can have tinned dog meat and like it!'

Jock Kennedy was a giant of a man. Hamish was equally tall but thin and lanky whereas Jock was broad-shouldered with a great bull-like head.

As he heated the pies and pulled out cans of beer and cans of dog food, Jock said in reply to Hamish's questions, 'We don't talk about them.'

'Stop talking havers. Who the hell is "them"?'

Jock leaned on the counter. 'The evil spirits.'

'A man like you!' jeered Hamish. 'Frightened of a lot of noises.'

Jock leaned right over the counter and whispered, 'You should see what they did to the kirk. Meenister, himself, was preaching against superstition. They come down frae the castle in the night and painted the altar table red wi' blood!'

Chapter Two

And things that go bump in the night.
Good Lord deliver us!
—Anonymous

'Why didn't he say so?' asked Charlie. 'I mean, he wants folk to think it's a lot of bollocks. That's straightforward, ordinary vandalism.'

Jock looked nervously around. 'What makes you think that?'

It was as if Jock's superstitious fears were making Charlie lose his own. 'See here,' said Charlie, 'Hamish and me are going to sleep in the tower tonight and we'll find out exactly who is playing silly buggers.'

'If you want to be safe, I'd go to the church this evening. Haggis preaches a good sermon.'

'Turned religious, Jock?' asked Hamish.

'The noises coming from that tower are enough to make a Protestant cross himself,' said Jock.

Outside the shop, Hamish and Charlie sat on a bench and ate their pies and drank beer while Hamish's dogs,

Lugs and Sally, reluctantly sniffed the dog food and ate only some of it.

'Och, the puir wee souls,' said Charlie. 'I'll get them a couple of pies.'

Left on his own, Hamish sent his highland radar out, feeling for oddities in the atmosphere. The wind had suddenly died and there was a dampness in the air. Hamish hoped it wouldn't rain, as there was no roof to the tower. He sensed a bad atmosphere; a *waiting* atmosphere. The villagers are waiting for something bad to happen, he thought. I'll maybe go to church this evening. Frightened people always end up in church. Everything was still and calm. Suddenly the wind came back. Ripples of waves ran down the long sea loch and sent clumps of sea pinks by the water's edge bobbing and nodding.

Hamish was seated in church that evening with Charlie, not listening at first to the reading because he was hoping that if there was a God, he would take care of his cat, Sonsie, that he had returned to the wild.

'Hot stuff,' he realized Charlie was whispering.

Peter Haggis was up in the pulpit, holding on to the wings of the brass eagle and reading from the King James Bible's version of the Song of Solomon. His voice, filled with passion, rose up to the circular stained-glass window.

'Let him kiss me with the kisses of his mouth: for thy love is better than wine.'

His eyes were burning and he seemed to know the words by heart.

'A bundle of myrrh is my wellbeloved unto me: he shall lie all night betwixt my breasts.'

He's directing all this at somebody, thought Hamish. With his height and from his pew at the back of the church, he saw that the target of the minister's fervour was probably the owner of the silky fair hair in the third pew from the front. Just suppose, Hamish mused, that if Haggis and that blonde are having an affair, maybe they meet at the tower and have a tape of screams and yells to scare people away. No, that's daft. They wouldn't hear anyone coming. I wonder what Christine wanted the red paint for. Back to the blonde. Now, if she's married to the man next to her, then trouble could be brewing. Aha, sister Sheila doesn't like all this Song of Solomon passionate reading. When she's not chewing her fingernails, she's looking at the blonde with sheer hatred.

Why is she stuck up here in this remotest part of the British Isles with her brother? What's the attraction?

The reading was over and the congregation rose to sing 'Oh, God from whom all blessings flow.'

The sermon was about loving thy neighbour as thyself, but Hamish thought cynically that the minister's thoughts were on carnal love rather than spiritual. He began to get angry. The church was full. All these villagers had come for a bit of spiritual comfort, but they may as well have attended a black mass.

20

He was so angry that he delayed leaving the church until every member of the congregation had shaken the minister's hand at the church door and left.

'Good evening, Officer. I trust you enjoyed our little service?'

'No,' said Hamish. 'There was damn all spiritual comfort. If you want to get into her knickers, keep it outside the church.'

'I don't know what you are talking about, but you are coarse and rude and I will report you.'

'Oh, please do,' said Hamish. He crammed his cap on his red hair and walked off.

'Now, ye shouldnae ha' said that,' said Charlie. 'Not like you to be vulgar.'

'I got angry,' said Hamish ruefully. 'This damn place always upsets me.'

'I notice you've been a wee bittie on edge lately,' said Charlie. 'Maybe you're going through what Archie claims is the men's men's paws.'

'Still too young. You have to be over forty and get a craving for a leather jacket and a Harley. There's something bad in the air. Well, Handy has invited us for supper. Wish we had someone like him in charge.'

'Why do you think he really wanted to retire up here?' asked Charlie.

'God knows. Mind you, it's had a couple of previous owners who've already done a lot of restoration on the eighteenth-century bit. Besides, it was probably as cheap as chips.'

* * *

Hamish approached the police station cautiously. Here I am, he thought, an officer of the law wearing a utility belt with Taser, spray, and restraints, and I'm scared of one woman. He would not admit guilt was causing the fear. His dogs ran ahead and through the large flap on the door. He stood outside the door. She wouldn't, would she? Would she have played that trick of balancing a pot of paint so that when he opened the door it would fall on him?

But the door was closed. Where could she balance it? He went in. The kitchen was clean and sparkling. The dogs were lapping at their water bowls. Hamish felt the tension leave his shoulders. He went into his living room and lit the fire. 'Oh, peace that passeth understanding,' said Hamish, stretching out his long legs to the fire. Sally, the poodle, jumped up on the sofa on one side of him and Lugs climbed up on the other.

'Damn,' muttered Hamish. 'I forgot to lock up the hens.'

He went out to the henhouse and shooed the birds in. He was about to shut the door when he saw a dim light shining at the back of the shed. He walked forward and bent down. The glow was coming from a small night-light in the shape of a blue pig. He picked it up and stood up. There was a cord attached to it. He gave it an impatient tug and then suddenly jumped aside as a pot of red paint tilted its contents down into the shed.

'Christine!' He shouted her name like an oath. His boots were spattered but at least his uniform jersey and trousers had been spared. Fortunately, it turned out to be emulsion paint. If it had been gloss, he would have had to spend a long time getting rid of it in case the fumes made the birds ill.

He was sure that Handy would not expect Charlie and himself to be in uniform so, back in the station, he changed into an old sweater and jeans, found a warm coat and hat, and rolled up his sleeping bag. Hamish decided not to take his pets with him. He knew that once home for the night, they usually slept until morning. He reluctantly put his utility belt on again. It got heavier and heavier every year, he thought sourly, as more gadgets were added to it.

He drove to the Tommel Castle Hotel where Charlie was waiting impatiently in the courtyard. 'George wanted to come with us,' said Charlie. 'Let's get out of here.'

'George' was Colonel Halburton-Smythe, owner of the hotel. Although devoted to Charlie, he showed signs of wanting to be a sort of Poirot. He was also in competition with Hamish Macbeth, the man who had been engaged to his beautiful daughter, Priscilla, and then had broken off the engagement. He wanted to show that Hamish was nothing more than a highland idiot with an undeserved reputation.

Charlie loaded a huge hamper in the back and then joined Hamish. 'What have you brought?' asked Hamish. 'Handy's going to feed us.'

'Some things I need,' said Charlie, folding his lips in a firm line.

Hamish told Charlie about the red paint. 'Women can get awfy petty,' said Charlie. 'Mind you, she didnae like those birds. Couldn't understand why you didn't put one in the oven. Nor could she understand why you didn't send your old sheep to the shambles.'

'I'll get around to it,' said Hamish sulkily.

When they arrived at Drim, the sun was just setting behind the tall jagged mountains that guarded the loch. Later on, in the summer, it would be light all night long. The evening air smelled of wild thyme, bell heather, salt, and tar. But Hamish suddenly stiffened on Handy's doorstep, like a hound scenting game.

'What's up?' asked Charlie.

Hamish shook himself. 'Chust a feeling. There's violence in the air. Maybe a storm coming.'

He rang the bell and Freda, Handy's sister, answered the door. Rather than the sulky, sullen dame of their previous visit, she smiled a welcome. 'He's in the drawing room,' she said. Her Glasgow accent was stronger than her brother's. She had thick brown hair, a small face, and small twinkling eyes. She walked in front of them, clumsily, on a pair of very high heels.

'I'm trying them out again,' she said, holding open the door of the drawing room. 'Heels, that is. If you stop wearing them, it's difficult to get used to them again. You walk like a man trying to look like a woman.'

Handy rose to meet them. He was wearing an expensive-looking tweed jacket, a white shirt, and a silk tie.

24

'I'm afraid we're no' suitably dressed,' said Hamish.

'You're dressed for ghost hunting and that's all that matters,' said Handy. 'Drink? Got a twelve-year-old malt.'

They both accepted crystal tumblers of whisky. Hamish looked around the drawing room and began to feel uneasy. He knew precious little about antiques but he recognized good old furniture when he saw it. Various pieces seemed to glow in the soft lamplight. The sofa he and Charlie were sitting on had deep feather cushions and was made of mahogany and basketwork.

'Sanitary towels, Hamish,' said Handy, looking amused.

For one mad moment, Hamish thought this was a new sort of oath.

'My dad was Lady Jane sanitary towels. Left a fortune to my brother, John, because Dad was furious at me going into the police force. Well, poor John died at his desk in the factory and the money all came to me. I'd got sick of the police force: the paperwork, the targets, seeing good men leaving because they couldn't stand it any more. So I got out. But I like working. I gave a lot of money to charity and bought this place with the idea of doing it over and selling at a profit. Freda's just getting over a nasty divorce.'

'Charlie and I went to the kirk this evening,' said Hamish. 'The minister was reading from the Song of Solomon with his heart in every word. So who is the blonde? I only saw the back of her head.'

'That'd be Olivia Sinclair, ex-model. Married to Selwyn Sinclair, owner of Sinclair Electronics.'

'But I mind the factory is over outside Tain,' said Hamish.

'Aye, but he lives in the old Carrington place. That big place on the Lairg road stuck in the middle of nowhere. Folk do say he bought it to keep his flirty wife out of playing games. I don't think she realized he was religious until she married him. Married last year. I'd give it a few months if he doesn't kill her first. Mind you, maybe he just drags her to the kirk out o' spite.'

Hamish shifted uneasily. 'Sometimes a woman can get a man so besotted that he'll do it for them. Murder, I mean.'

'Trouble is that sister, Sheila, fancies Selwyn, and that one is a red-hot bundle of passion with nowhere to go.'

'Oh, well,' said Hamish, 'a lot of folk come to the Highlands but one winter usually sees them off.'

'I know what you mean,' said Freda. 'My poor brother. But I can't take any more of this isolation. I'm off back to Glasgow next week. It's a good thing I have a generous brother because dear Daddy left me sod all.'

Peter Haggis was smouldering like the peat fire on his living room hearth. 'He beats her. I know it,' he said savagely. 'When she shook hands with me in the porch, her sleeve slid back and there was a great bruise on her arm.'

26

'She probably painted it on. She's working you up, you fool,' raged his sister. 'Her husband is a fine man and she's trying to break him.'

But Peter barely heard her. He clasped his hands in prayer. The firelight turned his eyes to gleaming red. Sheila, his sister, stared at him with a feeling of despair. She put on her coat and went outside. A sudden gust of wind whistled down the loch, sending ripples of dark choppy waves glittering with the reflections of the first stars racing towards the village. There was a drought in the Highlands. It hadn't rained for months. But bad weather was forecast. Sheila looked up at the sky. Above the craggy tops of the mountains, long fingers of black were beginning to stream in from the west. She felt worried and miserable. She had considered it her Christian duty to devote her life to her brother. But that was when he had a pleasant parish in Perth. Suddenly, he had decided to move to Drim of all places.

She reflected it had all started at the New Year's Eve ball in Perth two years ago. Olivia had been there, dazzling all the men. It was there her engagement was announced. It was also there that Sheila had seen her brother at one point in the evening, holding Olivia closely in a waltz, and afterwards looking completely dazed. Selwyn was a good man.

But she had forgotten about it until he suddenly announced he was moving to Drim. That was until Olivia began to appear in the village.

'Miss Haggis,' said a voice behind her, making her jump.

Sheila swung round. The man held the torch he was carrying up to his face.

'Mr Sinclair!' exclaimed Sheila.

After a good dinner, Hamish and Charlie settled into their sleeping bags on the floor of the tower. A loud whistling and moaning started up.

'Whit's that!' yelled Charlie.

'It's the wind getting up,' said Hamish. 'It's those arrow slits. Makes that moaning sound.'

'There's a creepy rustling sound!'

'Charlie, we're lying on piles and piles of dry leaves. The draught is moving them around. I don't like the situation in Drim.'

'The ghosts?'

'No, the minister and his sister. Now, Sheila Haggis is one walking time bomb.'

'Why? Plain wee biddie.'

'She's got beautiful eyes and a passionate mouth.'

'Hamish, I thought ye'd be ower the ladies for the moment.'

'I don't fancy her. But someone might. Go to sleep.'

'I cannae sleep. Do you think it might be the ghost of auld Mungo Mackay?'

'No!'

Mungo Mackay had been a Jacobite sympathizer. After Culloden, the castle had been set on fire and Mungo and his wife and son had perished in the flames.

They had gone to the top of the tower for safety. As the fire had not touched the attached living quarters, an English officer had moved in. He was found with his throat cut before his family could join him. Since then, it had had various owners.

Hamish woke in the morning. A hazy sun was shining down from a milky sky.

He sat up and nudged Charlie awake. 'There you are, Charlie,' said Hamish. 'No ghosts, only the wind up in those remaining arrow slits.'

'I don't think Handy would have dragged us up here if it was only the wind,' said Charlie. 'We didnae search for clues. I mean, folk in the village would know we were here.'

Hamish was thinking of bacon baps and hot coffee from the shop in Drim and said impatiently, 'What clues?'

Charlie started to walk up and down, scraping the leaves aside with his size twelve boots. He had almost reached one of the walls when he gave a great cry and disappeared through the floor.

Hamish rushed over. He stared down into the darkness. 'Charlie! Answer me! Are you all right?'

'Aye, I fell on sacks. Can you shine a torch down here? I havenae put my belt on.'

Hamish retrieved his own torch and shone it down into the hole. A broken flight of steps was revealed.

'I'm coming down,' he said. Hamish gingerly felt his way down the steps. When he reached the bottom, he swung his powerful torch round the place.

'We've got company, Charlie,' said Hamish.

'What!'

'There's a wee man over there and he's very, very dead.'

Chapter Three

Them that asks no questions isn't told a lie,
Watch the wall, my darling, while the Gentlemen go by.
                                                            —Rudyard Kipling

Hamish took out his phone. 'No signal here, Charlie. I'll use the radio in the car. Are you sure you didn't knock your head or anything?'

'I'm just bruised. Oh, sir, dinnae leave me here wi' a dead man.'

'Don't be daft. He's dead. He's not a ghost. I'll be back in a minute.'

But Hamish was much longer. He got a flask of coffee and two bacon baps from the shop and then made a call to police headquarters and then a call to Handy, telling him what had happened. He had forgotten how superstitious Charlie could be, but never did he expect to find him shaking with terror and half fainting.

'Pull yourself together, you great ox. Look! Coffee and baps.'

'He spoke to me,' said Charlie through white lips.

'What? The dead man?'

'No, the Mackay.'

A voice shouted down the hole, 'Can I come down?'

'I'm afraid not, Handy,' Hamish called back. 'It's a crime scene.'

'Do you know who it is?'

'No, although there's something familiar about the face. Not much decomposition. Middle-aged. Expensive sports jacket and cords. No sign of injury. But I daren't examine him. I'll photograph him with my phone. The pathologist and the full circus from Strathbane will be here soon.'

Hamish turned his attention back to Charlie. 'Dead men don't speak. You probably heard Handy.'

'Hamish, I heard him.'

'So what did he say?'

'He said, "You're doomed, laddie."'

'Did you see his lips move?'

'No, but . . .'

'No, but havers, you daft lummox. It's the fear talking to you. That is one very dead corpse. Let's see if we can find another way out of here. Come on, stand up. Now shine your torch around and I'll shine mine.'

Then Hamish exclaimed, 'There on the left. That pile of boxes looks new. Keep the torch on them until I shift them.'

'If Blair comes along, he'll have you for messing up a crime scene,' said Charlie.

'If you really did hear a voice, then there's another way in here,' panted Hamish, sending boxes crashing to the floor. 'They're full of stones. Yes, there's a door and it's new and there's a great padlock. I'll just pick it. Hold that torch steady.'

Hamish worked away at the padlock with a skeleton key, selected from a bunch he always carried with him. At last, it clicked open. The door turned out to lead to a low rocky passage, black as pitch. 'Bring the sandwiches and flask, Charlie,' said Hamish. They walked along it, crouched down, shining their torches, until they came to another door. Again, Hamish had to fiddle with a padlock. That door opened on piles of gorse bushes, piled up at the entrance. They kicked them aside and found themselves looking down at the remains of a landing stage on the loch.

'Smugglers again, I bet,' said Hamish bitterly. 'Had them here before. One of them must have gone along that tunnel and pretended to be a ghost to frighten you, Charlie.'

'If I get my hands on the bastard, I'll kick his teeth in,' said Charlie bitterly. 'Had me as feart as a bairn. There's Handy waving to us. Wait till he hears what we've found.'

'Not yet,' said Hamish. 'What do we really know about him? He could be corrupt. Let's sit down and eat our breakfast.'

They sat on the edge of the jetty, their great regulation boots mirrored in the black water below. When they had finished eating, Hamish said, 'We'd better find out who the missing man was.'

'There's something about him. You know ... I think I saw the cheil on the telly,' said Charlie. 'Let's be having a look at that photo you took.'

Hamish showed him the photograph. Charlie shook his big head. 'Funny that,' he said. 'Now I think I must have imagined it. If it's smugglers, we'll have put an end to their smuggling.'

'Maybe not,' said Hamish. 'They'll wait a few months and start up again. Let's go and join Handy.'

Hamish showed Handy a picture of the dead man. 'There's something familiar about him,' said Handy, 'but folk look different when they're dead.'

A police helicopter sailed into view and landed on the flat bit of shore by the loch. First to descend was Superintendent Daviot, but to Hamish's relief he was followed only by an elderly man he judged to be the pathologist, the official photographer, and his friend Detective Inspector Jimmy Anderson.

Daviot rushed forward to greet Handy. 'Maybe he's going to say, *Mr Ebrington, I presume*,' muttered Hamish, and Charlie let out an unmanly giggle.

'I wonder if you recognized me,' said Handy. 'We haven't met before, have we?'

'I think I saw you at one of the Edinburgh functions,' said Daviot, who had, in fact, looked up Handy's photograph on the Internet.

'It is beginning to rain,' came the testy voice of the

pathologist, 'or am I expected to stand here freezing my assets off?'

Daviot swung round and glared at Hamish. 'Why are you still standing there, Macbeth? Take Sir James Creedy to the body.'

'Chust waiting for orders, sir,' said Hamish amiably. 'I'll lead the way, Sir James. Not often we get the honour of your presence. I've read about your work.'

Jimmy followed behind, feeling crossly that he should have been the one ordered to take care of the pathologist.

Sir James was tall and thin with a high-bridged nose and a way of walking forward as if he were about to fall over. Hamish thought he looked like a heron.

'We've just discovered a passage,' said Hamish, 'which would be safer for you as the steps inside are a bit dangerous, but I'm hoping the forensic boys might find something there that can lead us to the murderer.'

They reached the hole in the floor. Hamish unhitched his torch and shone it down the broken steps.

'I'll need more light,' complained the pathologist. 'I'll wait for the forensic team. In the meantime, give me your torch so that I can look at the body from here.'

Sir James shone the torch down and then turned the beam to right and left. 'I don't see a body,' he complained.

'If you will allow me, sir,' said Hamish, taking back his torch. He gingerly made his way down the stairs

35

and shone the beam onto where he had seen the body lying. There was no body. He desperately searched to left and right.

'What are you doing?' shouted Jimmy from above. 'You're contaminating a crime scene with your great boots.'

'The body's gone,' wailed Hamish. 'Someone's stolen the body.'

Not only was there the misery of losing a dead body, but it turned out to be the one day the drought broke at last. Great gusty gales carrying slashing rain poured down between the mountains from the Atlantic.

Hamish fretted. He could only be glad that he had taken that photograph. He had sent it on to police headquarters in Strathbane. After an hour, the report came back. Hamish's dead man was a Professor John Gordon, who was fixated on the idea of there being no God. He travelled the country, ranting and raving as he gave lectures to that effect. He had been due to speak at an outdoor meeting in Golspie a week before, but had never turned up. Before that, he had preached on the non-existence of God at a meeting in Strathbane. His sermons were popular with the young and loathed by the old.

There had been smugglers in Drim before and Hamish was sure they were back again. Maybe the professor had been examining the ruin and had stumbled upon them and so they had killed him. But if that was the case, where was his car? Last seen, he was driving a Volvo.

Daviot was worried. He was now faced with the delicate task of interviewing a retired chief superintendent. Handy invited him into the hall, but kept him standing and curtly declared he had never seen the professor before, alive or dead. Daviot had brought Hamish, Charlie, and Jimmy as backup. He went on questioning Handy, asking about his movements during the past week. He stiffened as Hamish's gentle voice said, 'I was thinking that Mr Ebrington here would hardly have encouraged two police officers to spend the night in the tower if he had known anything about a dead body.'

'Should I even dare to suggest such a thing?' raged Daviot. 'Speak only when you are spoken to, Macbeth.'

'In that case,' said Handy coldly, 'why are you asking me what I have been doing for the last week and if I ever had any dealings with the dead man?'

'Simply routine,' snapped Daviot. 'Take over, Anderson. I'm taking the helicopter and Sir James back with me. I am sure Macbeth will run you back to Strathbane at some point. You and Carter are to spend the day questioning the villagers.'

He stalked out.

'Anyone like a dram?' asked Handy.

'Kind of you,' said Jimmy. 'I'll just get rid of these two.'

'These two are friends of mine, and when I last

looked, a squad of policemen had been drafted in to question the villagers.'

He led the way into the study and bent down and lit the fire which had already been set with coals and kindling. He served whiskies all round and then asked, 'What happened to the ferocious Detective Chief Inspector Blair?'

'Told not to come. Mr Daviot was frightened he might offend you,' said Jimmy.

'Pity,' said Handy. 'I was looking forward to putting that one firmly in his place.'

'From your experience, sir . . .' Hamish was beginning.

'Handy, please.'

'From your experience, before today did you sense anything wrong about the village?'

'I didn't suspect any villainy. I felt sure someone was playing tricks, playing at ghosts. But that distracted me. Anyway, it's now a case of find the smugglers, and you'll find your murderers.'

'I wonder what they were smuggling,' said Hamish.

'Drugs, possibly. If it had been cigarettes or booze, they might just have stunned him.'

'But we don't know how he died, do we?' asked Charlie.

'No, not even that,' said Hamish. 'I was frightened to even turn the body over in case I got accused of contaminating the crime scene.'

Handy looked with some amusement at Jimmy, who was sipping a rare old malt, his eyes half closed with pleasure. 'What about you, Mr Anderson?'

Jimmy hauled himself back from a dream country of bright fires and old malt whiskies by the barrel. 'They'll maybe move up the coast. Isn't Loch Drim a tricky place to get into, Hamish?'

'Aye, it'll take experienced sailors.' Hamish sat up. 'That means folk wi' local knowledge.'

'Or someone prepared to sell that knowledge and act as a pilot,' suggested Charlie.

'And someone local would know about the tower and about that secret passage,' said Hamish. He rose reluctantly to his feet. 'Charlie and I had better scramble along to the head of the·loch and see if there are any traces of them.'

As Hamish knew from previous experience, there was no path to the head of the loch. He and Charlie stumbled through the rain-slippery scree of the flanks of a mountain, finding relief in the occasional animal track. The wind was so strong and the rain so heavy, it was as if some giant were throwing buckets of water into their faces.

Hamish stopped suddenly. 'This is ridiculous,' he shouted. 'We'll not be able to see a thing what with the great waves and the rain. We'll come back when it's calmed down.'

On returning to the castle to report to Jimmy that he would be better doing some research on the backgrounds of various people on the computer, he learned that Handy's sister, Freda, had been going to Strathbane to do some shopping and Jimmy had begged a lift.

Hamish dropped Charlie off at the Tommel Castle Hotel. Once inside his station, he fed his dogs, stripped off, and had a warm bath. Dressed in casual clothes, he lit the fire in the living room and – cradling a mug of coffee, and with his dogs settled on the sofa on either side of him – turned his mind to the case of the disappearing professor.

But it had been a long and exhausting day and his eyes began to close, thinking how peaceful it was without Christine bossing him around.

Hamish was abruptly woken half an hour later by a banging on the front door. It couldn't be one of the locals, he thought. They knew to use the kitchen door, as the front door had been stuck fast with damp for ages. He shouted, 'Kitchen door round the side o' the station,' and then rose reluctantly to see who had come to disturb his peace. As he opened the door, he was dreaming of a law that would let one charge people who came crashing into one's life with disturbance of the peace.

Sheila Haggis stood on the doorstep, glaring up at the tall policeman with the flaming-red hair and the dreamy smile on his face. 'Let me in,' she snapped. 'I'm drookit.'

'Still raining, I see,' said Hamish. 'Give me your wet coat and come through to the living room.'

When she was seated in an armchair by the fire, she stared at him and said, 'The gossip in the village is that it is you who solves all the cases and lets Strathbane take the credit.'

Hamish said nothing, merely smiled vaguely and said, 'How can I be of help?'

'There is a woman called Olivia Sinclair. She chases men, even though her poor husband, Selwyn, does not seem to notice.'

'I can hardly tell Mrs Sinclair to stop flirting,' said Hamish.

'You can ask her what she was doing having lunch with Professor John Gordon two weeks ago in Inverness.'

'You saw them?'

'I didn't recognize him until I saw his photograph on the television news this evening. That was the man I saw her with. He was holding her hand.'

'I will call on her tomorrow and ask her about it,' said Hamish.

'Why not tonight?'

'It's far too late,' said Hamish.

Before he went to sleep, he wondered if he should tell Jimmy about this latest bit of information. But Sheila could have made it up out of spite. Better to take Charlie and see what the lady had to say for herself.

The rain had stopped the following morning as Hamish and Charlie drove out to interview Olivia Sinclair. And yet, thought Hamish, there was more to come, because the mountains were clearly etched and had that pressing-closer-and-nearer look. But for the moment, watery yellow sunlight shone down on the landscape, turning the one-track road to gold.

On a flat plain, hedged in by tall pillared mountains, lay the Sinclairs' home. What had possessed a prosperous businessman to live in such an isolated spot, wondered Hamish. A tussocky lane led up to a square stone building, some blocked-in windows showing it dated from the days of the window tax. Hamish guessed it had originally been some lord's shooting box. There was no garden at the front. A field of heather led almost to the front door, where a solitary rowan tree stood guard against evil spirits. Smoke was rising from one of the tall chimneys. A Range Rover, the latest model, was parked at the side of the house.

He and Charlie got out of the police Land Rover. Charlie yawned and stretched. 'The air is great,' he said. The landscape was very still. A curlew's plaintive call sounded from the heather.

Hamish rang the brass bell beside the heavy oak door. There was a long silence. He had not heard anyone approach, but he noticed there was a spyhole in the door and had a feeling of being observed. 'Police!' he called sharply, and the door swung open.

Hamish had only caught a brief glimpse of Olivia Sinclair in the dimness of the church and was prepared to find himself facing a dazzling beauty in the clear light of day. But Olivia was tall and very thin, almost to the point of anorexia. Her blonde hair, although skilfully tinted, was not natural. She was dressed in a man's checked shirt, tied at the waist over a pair of tight-fitting jeans. Olivia had a high-cheekboned face and wide blue eyes, the blue framed by a circle of black. Slav eyes, thought Hamish. Her mouth was large and she had collagen-enhanced lips.

'We have a few questions to ask you concerning Professor John Gordon,' said Hamish. 'I am Police Sergeant Hamish Macbeth from Lochdubh, and this is Constable Charles Carter.'

'Come in,' she said. 'I have just made some fresh coffee. We'll have it in the sitting room.'

The room into which she led them had that soulless feel left by a professional interior decorator. Everything was in shades of brown and gold. There was no clutter of books or magazines. They waited as she poured mugs of coffee, then she asked, 'Why are you here?'

'We have received a report that you were seen in an Inverness restaurant holding hands with Professor John Gordon.'

'Oh, is that who he was? He simply invaded my table, seized my hand, and said, "You are the most beautiful lady I have ever seen." I told him to get lost and he did. Real weirdo in my opinion. Who told you this? Oh, I know. The Haggis female. That repressed creature *lusts* after my husband.'

'And does the minister lust after you?'

'I don't know. A lot of men do, particularly in this god-forsaken place. But usually they go off and take their frustrations out on the nearest sheep.'

To Hamish's surprise, Charlie laughed. He looked at him. To his even greater surprise, Charlie was gazing at Olivia with adoration in his eyes.

'So you have never seen the professor before,' pursued Hamish.

'Nope. Can't help. You lost the body, didn't you? What a hoot.'

'So what restaurant did you meet the professor in?'

'Maggie's Heiland Hame. One of those downmarket macaroni-and-cheese places on Ness Bank.'

'And when exactly were you there?'

'Wait a minute. Selwyn insists on receipts for every-thing.' She disappeared and came back after a few minutes, holding out a receipt. Hamish took it.

'And I need a receipt for that,' said Olivia.

Hamish wrote one out and gave it to her. He sensed that inside she was laughing at him.

So when he and Charlie were back in the Land Rover, Hamish said, 'We'll just run down to Inverness and check this out.'

'But if the Inverness police catch us poaching on their territory, they'll report us,' said Charlie.

'We'll nip home first and change into ordinary clothes and take one of the hotel cars,' said Hamish.

'I don't see why we're bothering,' said Charlie huffily. 'We should be ower at Loch Drim looking for the body. That bonnie lassie had nothing to do with it.'

'Are you talking about Olivia Sinclair? She's a tarted-up bag o' bones.'

'With all due respect, watch your mouth, *sir*.'

'We are not going to quarrel,' retorted Hamish. 'I will go on my own.'

They continued their way in grim silence. At last Charlie gave a reluctant laugh and said, 'We'll go together. May as well both get into trouble.'

'Right you are,' said Hamish, brightening up.

Chapter Four

In the highlands, in the country places,
Where the old plain men have rosy faces,
And the young fair maidens
Quiet eyes.
                                    —Robert Louis Stevenson

Because of Charlie's friendship with Colonel Halburton-Smythe, they were given permission to borrow a hotel car. But the colonel, who fancied himself a detective, wanted to come as well.

'Can't allow it, George,' said Charlie soothingly. 'If we're caught by the Inverness police, we'd be in double trouble for bringing a civilian along. But you could drive ower tae Drim and hae a wee chat with the locals. Maybe you might even find that missing body.'

The colonel smiled happily and said he'd go right away.

'I know you'll probably disagree with me,' said Hamish, as they drove south and over the Black Isle towards

Inverness, 'but although Olivia Sinclair may be innocent and her story true, I feel she's up to something. I feel she's a born manipulator and there she is, stuck out in the middle of nowhere.'

'Well, everyone's innocent until they're proven guilty,' said Charlie sententiously.

As they drove into the multistorey car park and then began to walk through the town, Hamish reflected that somehow Inverness seemed to get bigger every year. Of course, there were so many Polish immigrants that a priest had to be brought over from Warsaw.

Hamish would not have been surprised to find that there was no Maggie behind the café-restaurant on the Ness Bank, but some East European. But there was a Maggie, a tough-looking Glaswegian called Margaret Finlay. Her hair was dyed that colour called aubergine and her pudgy face was crossed with little broken red veins. It was a dismal-looking place with plastic table-cloths and a grimy floor. Tattered posters advertizing out-of-date events decorated the walls. Even two sea-gulls perched on the window ledge had dirty grey feathers. Hamish explained who they were and what they wanted to find out. Margaret led them to a table in the corner and peered at the till receipt.

'I cannae remember her or him,' she said, shrugging her massive shoulders and releasing a great smelly cloud of body odour mixed with a cheap perfume. 'This place gets awfy busy.'

Hamish looked around. Apart from one old-age

pensioner gloomily eating a mutton pie, there were no other customers.

'Do you have security cameras?' asked Charlie.

'Whit? Me? Dinnae be daft.'

'Do you have a waitress?' asked Hamish.

'Had a girl but she walked out.'

'What was her name?'

'Alice something.'

'But you'll have employment records?'

'Didnae check on her. She asked for a job and I told her to get started and then she just walked off afore the end o' the day.'

Four builders came in and Maggie hurried off to serve them.

'I should have left it to Inverness,' said Hamish. 'We'd better go back and put in a report, but before that, we'd better get to the entrance to Loch Drim and see if there's any evidence of smugglers.'

'I hate the idea of scrambling along those mountain slopes,' said Charlie. 'And it's beginning to rain again.'

'Archie Maclean's not doing much,' said Hamish. 'We'll see if he can take us round.'

'Right. What about your dogs?'

'They'll be all right,' said Hamish. The fact was that since the departure of his beloved wild cat, he shied away from any strong feelings of affection. He also felt guiltily that to grieve so deeply over the loss of a pet who wasn't even dead was mawkish.

* * *

48

Colonel Halburton-Smythe's enthusiasm for detection was waning fast. The police, still questioning the villagers, had told him to keep away and not interfere in police business. He dared not even go near the tower, which seemed full of white-coated forensic figures. Cold rain was being driven on a blustery wind. The old deerstalker on his head was a sopping-wet lump of tweed.

He decided to call at the manse as a last resort. Surely the minister wouldn't slam the door in his face.

It was Sheila Haggis who answered the door to him. He introduced himself. To his relief, she was welcoming, inviting him into a living room and taking away his wet coat and hat to the kitchen to dry them.

'So,' she said, returning with a tray of mugs of coffee and a plate of biscuits, 'you chose a nasty day to make a social call.'

The colonel opened his mouth to say he was detecting but sensed he would probably get another rebuff and said instead, 'The reason for my visit was to offer you and your brother an invitation to dinner at the Tommel Castle Hotel, which I own.' He had learned a lot from Charlie and had suddenly remembered Charlie talking sympathetically about the Lochdubh minister, Mr Wellington. 'Folk always take their troubles to the minister,' Charlie had said, 'but they never wonder how he's getting on or what he thinks.'

'That's very kind of you,' said Sheila. 'But why us?'

'I suppose because nobody bothers to help ministers.'

Peter Haggis walked in. His sister introduced the colonel and explained the reason for his visit.

'I say, that's so kind of you,' said Peter eagerly. 'A friend of mine told me the food is very good.'

Sheila scowled, guessing that the friend had been Olivia Sinclair.

'What about this evening?' suggested the colonel.

'Well, yes,' said Peter. 'It gets a bit lonely, having no one of our class to talk to.'

The colonel hid his shock. Hamish Macbeth, who considered the colonel to be an arch-snob, would have been amused. As the colonel told Charlie later, one never expected ministers to be so uppity.

'You'll have to put us ashore somewhere,' shouted Hamish above the noise of the fishing boat's engine. 'Can you manage it?'

'It's low tide,' said Archie. 'See thon great flat rock at the entrance? You've got to jump for it. But you'll have to make your way back on foot. I've got the fishing and I cannae be waiting around for the next low tide.'

He and Charlie managed to jump on to the flat rock, but found themselves at the foot of a tall cliff.

'Is there no way round this?' said Hamish. 'We should have brought climbing equipment.'

'I may as well get ma feet wet,' grumbled Charlie. 'What with the spray and the rain, I'm fair soaked.'

He eased himself into the sea at the side of the great rock.

'See anything?' called Hamish.

50

'Aye,' said Charlie. 'You'd better phone and get a boat here quick. There's a dead body caught under the edge o' this rock.'

Hamish found that he could get a signal on his phone and called for urgent help, saying the tide was rising quickly.

'We'll need to lift the body on to the rock,' said Hamish.

'Okay,' said Charlie. 'Och, I hope bits dinnae fall off. Here he comes.'

'Aye, I've got him. Looks like the prof.'

Charlie and Hamish stood side by side on the rock, holding the dead body upright between them.

Hungry waves began to dash against the rock. 'We'll be drowned if they don't hurry up,' wailed Charlie.

They were almost giving up hope when a helicopter hove into view. The body had to be hoisted up first and then finally they were both rescued. The dead body was to be taken straight to the morgue at Strathbane. As Hamish looked down, he shuddered as a giant wave crashed into the rock they had been standing on.

They were dropped off in the car park at police head-quarters and a waiting ambulance took the body away. Then Hamish found to his fury that Jimmy had left instructions they were to go straight to Drim.

'Not until we're dried out. Let's see if we can get some transport to Lochdubh.'

But no police car was available. Hamish phoned for a taxi, planning to charge it on his expenses. He

51

dropped Charlie at the hotel and said he would meet him in Drim.

Hamish showered and scrubbed, feeling a smell of decomposing body sticking to him, although he felt sure it was his imagination, for what was left of the professor had taken a battering from the waves and bits of him had been eaten by the sea creatures.

He was reluctant to race back to Drim, feeling he had not had enough time to think. He made himself a bacon bap and a mug of coffee. He did not feed the dogs because Willie, the waiter at the Italian restaurant, had put a note through the door to say that both had eaten plates of osso buco. Could any of the villagers in Drim be involved? If it was smugglers and if it concerned drugs then some people could easily be roped in to help because of the promises of thousands of pounds in return. He remembered the case of a highland woman who had been caught at Gatwick airport with five pounds of cocaine in her suitcase. At her trial, she had sobbed that all she had wanted was money for a new kitchen.

Drugs were often brought in on some sort of large ship which would hove to off the Outer Hebrides. A small boat would go out and unload the drugs before speeding off to the mainland.

He went through to his office and phoned the coast-guard to find out if any strange vessels had been spotted

52

off the west coast. Nothing, he was told. Everybody accounted for.

His mobile phone rang. He reluctantly answered it. It was Jimmy. 'Where are you?'

'I'm in the station. Had to get out o' my wet clothes. I'm just about to leave.'

'Well, you and Charlie have to call at your pal, Handy, and soothe him. Blair tried to interview him in his usual way. Handy threw him out. Then he gets on to some high-up at Police Scotland and it's poor Daviot who gets the bollocking.'

'So what do you need me for?' asked Hamish. 'And isn't Charlie there yet?'

'Haven't seen him. But get over here, laddie. Daviot's on the warpath.'

'Why? Nothing to do wi' me.'

'Listen. Blair creeps up to Daviot and whispers in his ear that isn't it strange that an ex-chief-super should buy a castle in Scotland and live in the grand style? So your instructions are to look as if you are pouring oil on troubled waters but to ferret out where he got the money.'

Hamish opened his mouth to say that he knew where Handy's money came from, but decided to keep that bit of information to himself. It meant a comfortable visit and perhaps Handy knew more than he realized and wasn't aware of it. He phoned Charlie and explained why they were to visit the castle. 'I wonder if you would mind going yourself,' said Charlie. 'You see, George has invited the minister and his sister to dinner and I've

53

been asked to join them. It might be a good way of getting some more information out of them.'

'That's fine,' said Hamish. 'Have a good meal and ask chef Clarry for some bones for the dogs.'

Hamish decided to wear off-duty clothes because his uniform was still wet. He found a blue shirt and a striped tie, remembering with a pang that both had been presents from Priscilla. Their engagement was long over because of Priscilla's sexual coldness, but he still, in an odd way, hankered after her. A dark pair of cords and a venerable but respectable tweed jacket he had found in a charity shop completed the outfit.

Lugs put a large paw on his knee as if to remind his master that he was not looking after his dogs as he should.

'Oh, all right,' said Hamish, 'you can come as well. But don't blame me if he has you banished to the ruins.'

As he drove through the gusty rain, he wondered about the noises that had emanated from the tower. If it had been someone playing a recording, say, and shouting 'Boooo!' then no one would have been frightened.

When he arrived and found to his relief that his dogs were welcome as well, he settled down by the fire with a small whisky and asked, 'Can you describe the haunting sounds? How did they manage to frighten the village?'

'They scared me,' said Handy. 'It mostly sounded like the wind and then there would be a low moan and then a whisper that you had to strain to hear which said, "Death, death", and then the sounds became more like the wind. Very sophisticated, if you know what I mean.

I gather the forensic team have not yet found any evidence of any type of recording.'

'I can't help you with much,' said Hamish. 'I am kept out of the picture as much as my superiors can manage. The only reason I am here is that Blair offended you and you phoned someone high up and I am here to murmur sweet nothings in your ear.'

Handy surveyed Hamish curiously. How had this lanky policeman with the flaming-red hair and gentle face managed to survive so long?

'A bit o' cunning and a bit o' blackmail,' said Hamish, who had the odd talent of some highlanders of reading a person's thoughts.

Handy looked startled for a moment and then assumed he had spoken his thoughts aloud. 'Have you met the glamorous Olivia?'

'I wouldnae call her exactly glamorous,' said Hamish.

'What! That woman exudes sex and come hither, enveloping men in a force field.'

'I didnae notice. Maybe it's because I've just finished a relationship which ended in acrimony so it's like having had a flu injection. I'm going to be immunized for a bit.'

'And is your constable immune?'

'Oh, she won't bother with anyone as lowly as Charlie,' said Hamish.

The minister and his sister were taken aback to find that Charlie was a guest as well. Sheila Haggis, who read historical romances, assumed that Charlie was possibly an illegitimate son of the colonel's. Peter Haggis put the big policeman down as acting as a sort of bodyguard when he was off duty.

Peter said he would rather not drink alcohol and scowled when his sister defiantly said that she would like some wine. They were not handed menus. As the colonel's guests, they were expected to eat what he had ordered. It was unfortunate for them that the colonel occasionally liked to give Charlie a treat by ordering some of the policeman's favourite food. Faced with a main course of sausage and mash, Peter scowled furiously. The fact that the sausages were venison, and the rich wine sauce a gourmet's delight, went unnoticed. The minister regarded it as a social snub. Charlie, who had hoped to do some gentle questioning, found all his forays treated with abrupt sharp barks of 'No', or 'Don't care what a load of superstitious idiots think.'

And then just as Peter was sulkily drinking coffee and trying to stop, without success, his sister ordering brandy, a voice tinkled in their ears. 'Peter, darling. How sweet to meet you.' The speaker leaned forward and kissed him on the cheek. The men struggled to their feet. Sheila leaned back in her chair and nursed her brandy goblet to her bosom.

Olivia was wearing a blue cashmere dress which clung to her figure. Her long legs were encased in sheer black tights ending in high-heeled strapped sandals. The minister looked as if he were lit up from within. Sheila scowled. 'Where is your husband?' she demanded.

'Oh, Selwyn is in the bar talking boring business. I saw you after I'd been to powder my nose. Much more entertaining, I thought. Please sit down. Mind if I join you?' And without waiting for an answer, she dragged a chair from a neighbouring table, placed it next to Charlie, and sat down. 'I haven't met this gentleman before,' she said.

'This is Colonel Halburton-Smythe, the owner of the hotel,' said Peter. 'He kindly invited us to dinner.'

'A dinner to which you were not invited,' said Sheila.

'Oh, my dears. How rude of me.'

'No, no, lady,' said the colonel. 'Delighted to meet you.'

'I am Olivia Sinclair. We've got a place at Tinerty.'

'Tinerty is nowhere,' said the colonel. 'Doesn't a sophisticated lady like yourself find it a bit lonely?'

'No. Always people around.'

'Do order something.'

'Ate already, but thank you.' She turned to Charlie. 'Are you here on duty?'

'Oh, no,' said Charlie awkwardly. 'I am a guest.'

'How very democratic!'

The little colonel bristled up. No one can be offended by snobbery more than another snob. 'Charlie is a friend of mine.'

'And where is your wife? Or are you not married?'

'Visiting friends.'

She's like a calculating machine, thought Sheila. The adoration has left the copper's eyes to be replaced with

57

speculation. Olivia placed a hand on Charlie's arm and smiled up at him. 'You think I'm some sort of a bitch. Confess! It's just that policemen frighten me.'

Before Charlie could reply, Sheila said harshly, 'The only people who are afraid of the police are people with something to hide.'

'Now, not true. But people like you always have such dire thoughts about people like me. Do you know why? The only exciting drama you have ever had in your life was when your angel cakes failed to rise in the oven.'

'I'm off to find better company,' raged Sheila, throwing down her napkin and storming off.

'I can only apologize for my sister,' said Peter. 'All this business about the dead professor has upset her.'

'Don't worry,' said Olivia. 'Your sister's found a great excuse to go and cry on my husband's shoulder.' The minister gazed at her with adoring eyes.

'What was the professor like?' asked Charlie. 'I mean, you met him.'

'I told you. I thought he was just some sort of nut.'

'You actually met him!' said Peter.

'Yes, my dear haggis pudding. I was in some sort of greasy spoon in Inverness and he came right up to me and said I was lovely and I told him to take a hike and that's all there is to it.'

Suddenly, Olivia set herself to please. She praised the colonel on his beautiful hotel and grounds and she sympathized with Peter over his 'lonely' life and begged him to call. She found out Charlie was originally from the Outer Hebrides and asked him many questions about the life there. At last Olivia rose and said she must rescue her husband. Charlie felt a note being pressed into his hand.

After he had thanked the colonel for dinner, Charlie made his way downstairs to his flat and quickly read the note. 'Come and see me tomorrow at ten in the morning. Don't tell anyone. Please. Olivia.'

Now, what's she up to? wondered Charlie, trying to be cynical and yet beginning to feel excited. He found Olivia dangerously attractive. To him, she looked like those models in the glossy magazines you saw in the doctor's waiting room. And there had been no real questions asked during dinner. He would phone Hamish in the morning and say he was feeling unwell.

Hamish was driving back to Lochdubh after a pleasant evening. He had been invited to stay for dinner. Freda had turned out to be amusing but said she couldn't wait to leave Drim. On the following morning, he planned to send Charlie back to Drim while he himself would go up the west coast, searching various inlets to look for traces of smuggling.

While he was in Handy's company, Hamish found himself liking and trusting the man. But once he was out of his genial orbit, doubts set in. He should check that the money had indeed come from sanitary towels. Perhaps, he thought uneasily, the very subject had been picked to deflect enquiries, for who but an honest man would choose to claim such an embarrassing source of wealth?

Morning brought Charlie's phone call, saying he felt unwell and thought it might be flu. Hamish told him to stay in bed, but was not overly concerned, assuming all Charlie had was a bad cold from the drenching in the sea the day before. But the fact that he once more had the whole police station to himself delayed his departure and he happily pottered about, repairing a leak in the henhouse and checking on his small flock of sheep.

He was enjoying himself so much that he began to wonder why on earth he should hanker after getting married. But maybe there was some woman out there who wouldn't mind the idea of a truly unambitious man. The rain had stopped but it was one of those grey days in the Highlands of Scotland when all colour seemed to have drained out of the landscape. No waves stirred on the sea loch, and a thin mist curled round the skinny boles of the forest trees on the other side.

He was about to follow his dogs into the police Land Rover when he heard himself being hailed by Mrs Wellington, the minister's wife.

'You have brought shame on the village,' she shouted. 'Shame!'

'If ye don't mind, Mrs Wellington. I'm busy.'

'Oh, yes. Off to look for another poor lady to seduce and cast off.'

Hamish sighed. The minister's wife had been joined

by the Currie sisters, their glasses almost steamed up with curiosity.

'Ladies, I was the one who was cast off,' said Hamish piously. He took a large handkerchief out of his pocket and blew his nose. 'Excuse me. I cannae talk about it.'

He jumped into the driver's seat and drove off, leaving the three women staring after him with baffled looks on their faces, like three foxes balked of their prey.

Hamish suddenly slammed on the brakes on the other side of the humpbacked bridge that led out of the village. Charlie! What was he up to? Charlie was never ill, nor was he lazy. But he had got into woman trouble before and he had been smitten by Olivia.

Hamish set off again and drove into the car park of the hotel. He was waylaid by the manager, Mr Johnson. 'If you're looking for young Carter, he's gone off somewhere.'

'Was a woman called Olivia Sinclair here last evening?'

'Selwyn's missus. Yes, she joined the Haggises and Charlie for dinner.'

'Thanks.'

Hamish drove steadily in the direction of the Sinclair home. He wondered just what Olivia was up to. Certainly women found Charlie attractive with his fair hair, blue eyes, and gentle manners. Maybe she had something to hide. If she got Charlie in her coils, she could find out how far the case was progressing.

The rain began to fall heavily, and a thick mist rolled down from the mountains. He slowed to a crawl, the windscreen wipers performing their metronome strokes, almost hypnotic. And then columns of mist began to weave and writhe in front of him as a little breeze arose, and, just as suddenly as it had descended, the mist rolled up the mountains, the rain stopped, and a glimmer of sunlight shone on the drenched countryside.

There in the distance appeared the Sinclairs' home, and he could see Charlie's battered old car outside.

'Come upstairs,' Olivia was saying to Charlie. 'There's something I would like you to see.'

Charlie cocked his big head to one side. 'I hear a car coming,' he said 'Are you expecting your husband home?'

Olivia quickly fastened the top two buttons of her blouse which she had earlier undone to show some cleavage. She jerked open the door and looked up at Hamish Macbeth.

'What do you want, Officer?' she demanded.

Hamish smiled. He was tempted to say, *Please may I have my constable back*, like a small boy asking for a stray ball that had landed in a neighbour's garden.

'I need to speak to Constable Carter,' he said.

Charlie loomed up behind her. 'What are you doing here?' he asked.

'Looking for you. More to the point, what are you doing here?'

'Och, I just suddenly thought of something import-ant,' said Charlie.

Here it comes, thought Hamish, knowing that every highlander has the talent of lying in his DNA.

But Charlie surprised him. 'I was just working up to asking Mrs Sinclair what a lady like herself was doing in a dump like Maggie's when Inverness is full of smart places to have coffee.'

'And?'

'I haven't asked her yet.'

'And what is your reply, Mrs Sinclair?' asked Hamish.

'My reply is – bugger off the pair of you and mind your own business or I will inform your superiors of police harassment.'

'But you invited me,' protested Charlie. 'You said you had something interesting to show me upstairs.'

'I said nothing of the kind!' shouted Olivia.

Charlie sighed and held up a small tape recorder. 'I have it here. Would you like me to play it for my sergeant?'

Olivia crumpled and burst into tears. Hamish was sure they were tears of rage and frustration but Charlie lumbered forward and took her in his arms. 'There, there,' he said. 'You tell Charlie all about it.'

'I'll wait for you at the end of the drive,' said Hamish.

But it was over half an hour before Charlie got into his car and drove to meet Hamish.

Hamish saw Charlie's face was glowing and there was a mark of lipstick on his cheek.

'I should have stayed,' said Hamish. 'I bet she told you it was her man's idea to stick her out in the wilds and that they haven't had sex in ages and she gets so lonely and . . .'

'All right!' shouted Charlie, his face flaming. 'Let's chust drop it.'

'Look,' said Hamish. 'We've got work to do. Instead of going to Drim, leave your car at the hotel and come with me up the west coast and let's see if anyone spotted anything suspicious.'

Hamish decided to ignore the whole matter of Olivia for the present. For Charlie to tape-record what she said meant a Charlie who was not all that willing to be taken in. But would Olivia leave Charlie alone? On a previous case, a high-ranking police officer had risked her job and her marriage in pursuit of Charlie.

But at the hotel, after Charlie had climbed into the passenger seat and had thrown a couple of bones to the dogs in the back, Hamish couldn't resist asking, 'Did you get anything useful out of Olivia?'

Charlie's normally smooth brow creased in thought. 'Just an impression, mind. Sort of as if she had on a flirty mask and behind it she was frightened.'

'Maybe we'll get Inverness police to take a closer look at Maggie's. Damn. I should ha' told them in the first place.'

'Tell Jimmy.'

'Too late. Inverness police will go to Maggie's and the fragrant Maggie will tell them about our visit.'

'What about that pal of yours?'

'Mungo Davidson? I didnae bother because I heard a couple o' weeks ago that he was on holiday. First stop,

I'll call him. Let's start off at Cromish. Sadie Mackay in the village shop might have heard something.'

'That's where Anka used to do the baking,' said Charlie. 'When's the wedding?'

'Next month. I'm to be best man. Dick's complaining that Anka has so many Polish relatives coming here for the wedding, there won't be room enough for all of them.'

Anka, an attractive Polish woman, was to marry Dick Fraser, Hamish's ex-constable turned successful baker. Hamish could still not understand how the dumpy Dick had managed to capture such a beauty.

They drove into the small village of Cromish and parked outside the shop. Hamish got out and stretched. Then he let the dogs out and watched them chasing each other round in circles. 'Sonsie used to do that,' said Hamish, remembering his wild cat. 'Used to play with Lugs. Oh, well.'

He choked back an impulse to cry and followed Charlie into the shop. 'It's yourself, Hamish!' cried grey-haired Sadie. 'And who will this be? My, you're a giant of a fellow.'

Hamish introduced Charlie. 'We'll be buying some stuff for our lunch.'

'I've got a wee bit o' mackerel for your cat.'

'I sent her back to the wild. Still got baps?'

'Aye, Anka sends up a big bag of frozen ones and that keeps me going.'

'Before we start shopping,' said Hamish, 'you'll have heard about the dead professor?'

65

'Aye, shocking. God's judgement on the poor wee man.'

'I'm afraid it was human judgement and we think it may be the work of smugglers. Have you heard any whispers about cheap cigarettes or booze being smuggled in?'

'Not a thing. Now, what can I get you? What about a couple o' sausage baps?'

The days had turned fine so they took their lunch down to the beach, where great glassy green waves rolled in from the Atlantic. 'Good sausage,' said Hamish. 'Is there anywhere outside Scotland that has square sausage?'

'Don't think so,' said Charlie. 'She was lying, wasn't she?'

'I'm afraid so,' said Hamish. 'Oh, it'll be a man in a van wi' cheap booze or cigarettes and times are hard for the small shopkeeper. I could get a search warrant and come back, but I'll finish eating and then suggest it might be easier if she just told me about it and that way we can keep her out of court.'

'I don't think smugglers would use Cromish,' said Charlie. 'Looks too open.'

'There are caves and cliffs just round that end,' said Hamish. 'I nearly forgot Mungo. I'll give him a call.'

Mungo listened carefully as Hamish talked about Maggie's and Olivia's visit. 'What we want to know is what a rich and sophisticated lady and a daft professor were doing in a dump like that. I know I should ha' told you. Please don't let them know I was on their patch.'

'Don't do it again, you wanker,' said Mungo. 'Now, here's the thing. We've had plainclothes in at Maggie's, slurping her lousy coffee and eating the salmonella special, and found out sod all. You see, there's been whispers o' drug dealing going on there. Anyway, I'll let you know. Off the record, of course. And in return, next time I'm up your way, you can buy me and my fiancée dinner.'

'Fiancée! But you're married.'

'Got the divorce last year. This will be wife number three.'

'Good luck wi' this one,' said Hamish.

He rang off and turned to Charlie. 'Finished? Then let's get the dogs back in the Land Rover and go and make one wee body's life a misery. Maybe we'll try the back door o' the shop first.'

At the back of the shop was a battered old Ford van. Sadie and a tall pimply youth with ginger hair were loading a box into the back of it.

Her normally rosy cheeks turned white when she saw Hamish. 'I'll chust be having a wee keek into those boxes, Sadie,' said Hamish.

'Get a warrant, pig,' said the youth.

Hamish ignored him. 'Sadie,' he said gently, 'I can get a warrant and Charlie will go and get it and I will wait right here until it arrives. If I find what I think I'm going to find and have applied for a warrant, I will need to charge you with a crime and I don't want to do that.'

'Ah'm telling you, man, you creep me out,' said the youth.

'Oh, change the TV channel inside your weak brain,' said Hamish. 'Sadie? Come on, lass, what's it to be?'

'Go home, Geordie,' said Sadie.

'I am afraid Geordie stays right here,' said Hamish. Geordie stepped forward swinging his fists. Charlie picked him up as if he were a small child, and placed him on top of a crate, saying, 'Sit there and shut up.'

Geordie burst into tears and between gulps and sobs said he did not want to go to prison where he would be made to 'peddle his ass'. Despite the boy's height, Hamish judged him to be no more than fifteen.

Sadie scrubbed her eyes with her apron and said wearily, 'Go ahead. It's just cigarettes. I haven't sold any yet.'

Hamish opened a box she pointed to and stared down at it in surprise. 'Sadie, these are e-cigarettes. These are the things people use to give up smoking.'

'It was just one box,' said Sadie. 'They normally cost about twenty pounds each and he was letting me have them for ten.'

'And what did he charge for the stuff to put in them?'

'What stuff?'

'You get little bottles of either nicotine flavour or fruit flavour and they fill up thon little wells near the top.

68

Anyway, I'll need to confiscate this. I'm after smugglers, Sadie, not two-bit chancers. Why did you do it?'

'After Anka left, people stopped coming from all over. It wasn't just her baps but her cakes, you know. And even up here, business rates and taxes are miserable. He said people'd go mad for these. But after I'd bought them, I felt so guilty, I did not want to put them out for sale.'

'Keep them out the back and don't try to sell them,' said Hamish. 'When was this?'

'About three weeks ago.'

'Have you a security camera in the shop?'

'I'll look for you, Hamish, but I play over a lot of the disks. It was only three weeks ago about five in the evening so I might still have it.'

Sadie had not used the relevant disk again and Charlie and Hamish took it out to the Land Rover where they slotted it into Hamish's computer. They ran it forward to around five in the evening and waited. Then a small squat man came in and leaned over the counter. 'That's Fatty Crumm,' exclaimed Charlie.

'Who's Fatty Crumm?' asked Hamish.

'He lives down in one of those tower blocks by the docks,' said Charlie. 'Petty thief. But not violent.'

'We'll pay him a visit. I'll go and calm Sadie down and tell that silly boy to keep his mouth shut while you get this Fatty's address.'

'I'll have a word wi' Jimmy, but when we're practically on Fatty's doorstep or he'll try to get in there first and keep us out. Aren't you worried one o' the villagers might blab about the contraband? I mean, the idiot child, Geordie?' asked Charlie.

'Doesn't matter if he talks. They'll all clam up to protect Sadie.'

Jimmy had arranged to meet them down at the docks in a café that made Maggie's look posh. 'I'm not pleased with you,' began Jimmy angrily. 'We get a call from Mungo Davidson in Inverness that Olivia Sinclair was seen in Maggie's café with none other than the dead prof. So I get out to the middle o' nowhere and ask the lady. She says huffily she told you all about it.'

'So she did,' put in Charlie quickly. 'It was when I was having dinner at the hotel that she came up to our table and we got talking.'

'And ye never thought to call me?'

'He told me,' said Hamish. 'Tried to get you. Your phone must be on the blink or you were in a dead area.'

Jimmy had indeed been in a 'dead area'. That was, he was in a pub with his mobile switched off.

'Well, let's get going and see if Crumm is at home,' said Jimmy. 'I havenae told Blair what we're up to because there may be nothing in it and I don't feel like pinching small-time villains today.'

Fatty lived in Atlee Towers. What on earth were the town planners thinking of when they had these monsters thrown up to be filled with the scum of the earth? Their children vandalized the lifts, painted the walls with graffiti, and shit in the passageways. Anyone with any claim to decency would have been driven out long ago.

The tall tower building was full of the noise of the rising wind. As Hamish guessed, the lift was broken. 'What number?' asked Jimmy.

'Three hundred and four,' said Charlie.

'Here we go then,' said Jimmy. 'You pair go and get him and bring him to headquarters for a wee chat.'

'Haven't got a warrant to arrest him,' said Hamish. 'Och, the climb up the stairs'll do you good.'

Jimmy groaned. He was a wiry, foxy-faced man who loathed exercise. He had reached the first landing when Charlie called, 'This is odd.'

'What's odd?' asked Jimmy. 'Or do you plan to wait down there all day?'

'Usually the big numbers are up on top. But here, they're on the ground floor,' said Charlie. 'There's a board here and you can just make it out under the graffiti.'

'Great!' said Jimmy. 'Now let's hope he's at home.' Jimmy was anxious to get the interview over with as soon as possible. He knew he should have kept Hamish and Charlie in Lochdubh and brought a detective instead. But Hamish in the past had, through his odd intuition, a way of seeing round corners.

Fatty was at home. Charlie thought it was more like the lair of a junk-food animal. His small living room was crammed with discarded wrappers and pizza boxes. Soft-drink cans were lined up along the mantelpiece and spilled over onto the already cluttered floor.

The smell was dreadful. Jimmy opened the window wide. 'I'll catch ma death,' whined Fatty. His real name was Chester Crumm. But his vast size earned him the nickname of Fatty. He had a round face and several chins. His sparse hair covered parts of a scruffy scalp. His clothes were stretched across his bulk.

'Now, Chester,' began Jimmy who had no intention in these PC days of using that nickname. You never knew when people might be taping you on their smart-phones. 'It has come to our attention that you have been peddling contraband goods in Cromish.'

'I don't even know where that is,' whined Fatty.

'You went into the village shop and sold a case of e-cigarettes and we've got it on video.'

'It was give tae me,' said Fatty righteously. 'Man down at the docks, he says, "Here you are. Cigarettes. Make yousel' a bob."'

'And what did this generous gentleman look like?' asked Hamish.

'Medium height. Ordinary clothes. Looked like a seaman aff one o' the tankers. They aye hae that bandy-legged walk.'

'Come on,' sneered Jimmy. 'Do you expect us to believe this rubbish?'

'Unless it was right before the Customs men were about to arrive,' said Hamish.

'That's right. They was all ower the place so I scarpered. I thought maybe I'd better try to sell the stuff as far away from Strathbane as I could. But, man, e-cigarettes. It's the real ones folk want.'

72

'They might be faulty,' said Hamish. 'I mean, I've never heard of really cheap e-cigarettes being sold in Europe. Wasn't there something in the paper about some e-cigarettes setting the place alight when you try to charge them?'

'Can you take a guess at the name o' the ship the man might have come off?' asked Jimmy.

'Maybe it was the *Baltic Queen*,' said Fatty. 'Thon's the last ship's been in here. I mean nothing much berths here.'

'Keep your mouth shut about this and we won't be charging you,' said Hamish quickly.

'And why not charge him?' demanded Jimmy when they left.

'Because it would all lead back to Sadie and the poor widow would get a criminal record. Also, it might alert the real smugglers.'

'I'll leave it for now. We'd best track down this *Baltic Queen*. Get back to your beat, Hamish, and don't come sniffing around here again.'

'Ungrateful bastard,' said Hamish. 'I'm hungry again.'

He stopped at a fish-and-chip shop and bought fish and chips for himself and Charlie, and haggis suppers for the dogs. They went up on the moors to eat in peace. The fickle Sutherland weather was changing again, heralded by three rainbows stretched across the flanks of the mountains.

'It must be the only place in the British Isles where you can see three rainbows at once.'

'Aye, it's a bonnie sight,' said Charlie, munching contentedly.

Charlie was a good man, reflected Hamish, but sometimes he missed Dick. Dick had been a combination of camper and caterer. Every stop and out would come the stove, the picnic table, and a supply of goodies. But Hamish's mood grew darker. What was it that Dick had that he did not? He blushed as he realized he had voiced his thought aloud.

'Baps,' said Charlie. 'Congress cake, fairy cakes, fern cakes, you name it. That's Dick's passion and Anka shares it down to the last crumb. An English pal of mine once said to me, "I've got to bring back those Scottish rolls. What are they called? Baps, that's it." And it's like the days when folk used to say cheesecake isn't what it used to be. Everyone'll tell you that baps aren't what they used to be, except for Anka's. Imagine a Pole showing the Scots how to bake.'

'It's happening all over,' said Hamish. 'The South Koreans have just won the Best Baguette competition in Paris.'

Charlie laughed. 'Maybe that's what drove the poor prof to stop believing in God. You know, if there's a God, why can't I get a decent bap?'

Hamish sighed. 'We'd better get on. I know: Let's try

Handy. Surely an ex-copper, however high up, must have kept his nose for villains.'

But Handy was not at home, and neither was his sister.

'Let's call on Sheila Haggis,' said Hamish. 'Maybe she's got some more tips.'

'Look ower there,' said Charlie. 'That's her just leaving.'

Hamish started to run. He was a champion hill runner and soon caught up with Sheila as she was just letting in the clutch.

She opened the car window. 'What is it?' she demanded. 'I'm busy.'

Hamish told her what Olivia had said, and Sheila sneered. 'And you believed that rubbish! Men!'

'And what were you doing down at Maggie's?' asked Hamish.

'You stupid man. I'd just gone for a walk along the river. Now get out of my way.'

She drove off just as Charlie came ambling up to join Hamish. 'What's up?' he asked.

Hamish had a blind look in his hazel eyes. He focussed on Charlie and said slowly, 'What would take a professor, a minister's daughter, and a classy beauty to Maggie's?'

'Drugs?'

'Could be.' Hamish pushed back his cap and scratched his fiery hair. 'Let's find out who's the doctor for this village. We'll ask Jock.'

Jock volunteered that they had to go to a Dr Farham in Braikie. Emergencies were dealt with by the ambulance service. 'And a lot of folk here use the ambulance service,' said Jock, 'because when you phone for an appointment, you're told the wait is three weeks.'

'So Braikie it is,' said Charlie as they drove off. 'Are we going to call in on Dick?'

'Why not?'

Dick and Anka had transformed their living quarters above the shop into offices. They had bought a house outside of the town. Hamish had found himself hoping that Anka might have become 'a wee bit dowdy', a phenomenon he had noticed before in married women. Not that Anka was married but she and Dick had been together for some time now. But Anka, from her long legs to her auburn hair and green eyes, was as dazzling as ever.

Ever since they had put their famous bakery items for sale online, they had done a brisk trade, employing girls to serve in the shop and two youths to help cope with the orders on the computers.

Dick had kept a small room above the shop for visitors. He bustled about, making tea and bringing in a selection of cakes.

'I'll take some of your baps back with me for the hotel,' said Charlie.

'No need for that.' Dick grinned. 'We supply them with breakfast baps. Big order. And if they need a special cake for someone's anniversary, we do that as well.'

Hamish told Dick all about the case while Dick folded his hands over his stomach and listened carefully.

When Hamish had finished, Dick said, 'I think it might be drugs, but I'd leave the *Baltic Queen* alone. That was probably some daft East Europeans trying to peddle cheap Chinese e-cigarettes. Could be some of the dangerous ones that were once on the market. You try to charge them and your house goes on fire. Only an idiot would buy one now. Speaking of idiots, how's our friend Blair?'

At that moment, Chief Detective Inspector Blair was hanging out of his living room window, screaming, 'Help!'

A burly neighbour, whom Blair detested, climbed up a ladder, heaved Blair out, and carried him down in a fireman's lift to cheers from the watching crowd.

A fire engine raced up followed by an ambulance and a police car. They would find out that the e-cigarette he had bought in a pub had gone up in flames when he had tried to charge it. It was his day off and he had been stretched out on the sofa, fast asleep, only waking when he fell off the sofa in the middle of a nightmare and found the place ablaze. Mary, his wife, had been out shopping. He would need to put the blame on her, say she had bought it, or he would be damned for having been stupid enough to buy anything at all offered cheaply in a pub. With that decision, he pretended to faint.

Hamish and Charlie waited patiently in Dr Farham's waiting room. Hamish wondered if anything had been done to it during the last hundred years. The walls were painted institutional green and the wood skirting, dark brown. A black marble fireplace held dusty orange crepe paper. A sampler with the legend HIS EYE IS ON THE SPARROW decorated one wall and on the other was a steel engraving of John Knox preaching in St. Giles Cathedral to a distinctly tarty-looking Mary, Queen of Scots. A grim-faced receptionist had told them they had to wait with such force and venom that the two large policemen sat down in hard chairs like obedient children.

'She shouldnae dye her moustache blonde,' whispered Charlie.

'Who? The gestapo at the desk?' whispered Hamish. 'It shows there's something up with her hormones, so go carefully or she'll be chasing us down the street with a hypodermic needle.'

Charlie let out a snort of laughter. The receptionist glared at him and said, 'There are ill people here. So kindly behave yourselves!'

'This is Monday,' whispered Hamish, 'and this room is full o' the society of the bad back. Turn up regular on Mondays. Oh, the last one's just gone in. Shouldn't be long now.'

At last, the final patient came out. 'Wait!' ordered the receptionist. She disappeared into the surgery and then emerged to say triumphantly, 'Doctor isn't able to see you. He's been called out on an urgent appointment.'

She barred the door to the surgery. Hamish lifted her to one side as she screamed and yelled.

78

He and Charlie walked in. Dr Farham was taking a slug of something from a silver flask as they entered.

'Now, aren't you the bad man,' said Hamish as he and Charlie sat down in chairs on the other side of the desk.

'I'm tired,' said the doctor huffily. He was a tall, thin man with a beaky nose and thick grey hair. 'I didn't know you were policemen. I told Miss Harricote that I could not see any more patients as it was already well over time for the day's surgery.'

'Harricote being the mean bean outside?'

'If you mean my excellent receptionist, yes. So what brings you?'

'Can you tell me if you have been treating anyone from, say, Drim for drug abuse?'

'Any patient's treatment is confidential.'

'I can get a warrant,' said Hamish, although he was sure he could not.

'Well, we'll wait until then. Good heavens, man! You should know a doctor cannot discuss his patients. How would you like it if I told the world you had AIDS?'

'And as I don't, it's all hypothetical,' said Hamish. 'I'll be back.'

'Dear me. The highland answer to Arnold Schwarzenegger.'

'Do you think we can get a warrant?' asked Charlie when they were outside.

'On a hunch? Not a hope. But we can bluff. Let's go and have a wee word wi' Sheila Haggis.'

The mercurial weather of Sutherland had turned cold. 'Lambing blizzard coming up,' said Hamish. 'Always seems to hit just when you think spring is here to stay.'

'Aye, it's purple-black ower to the west,' said Charlie. 'Let's get it over with. I don't want to be stuck in Drim for the night. Thon place fair gies me the creeps.'

'Charlie, when we get to Drim, would you mind giving the dogs a run?'

'We'll stop on the road,' said Charlie. 'I don't think you should see Sheila on your own. She could cry rape or something.'

Hamish agreed. He waited impatiently after they had stopped halfway to let the dogs out, glancing uneasily at the blackening sky to the west. Anxious to get going, he whistled them back into the Land Rover and set off for Drim just as the first flakes of snow came hurling across the windscreen.

By the time they had pulled up outside the manse, the snow was thick on the ground. 'How are you going to approach it?' asked Charlie as Hamish rang the doorbell.

'In the good old highland way,' said Hamish. 'Lie through my teeth.'

The door swung open and Sheila stood there. 'Come in,' she said. 'What brings you? In fact, if you haven't arrested that bitch yet, I don't really think I have time to speak to you.'

80

'Oh, this'll interest you,' said Hamish.

'Well, stop looming over me and come through to the kitchen. There's a good fire in the Raeburn.' They took off their caps and followed her. To Hamish's surprise, it was a friendly, cheerful contrast with the rest of the gloomy manse. An old Welsh dresser filled with Crown Derby plates decorated one wall, another held book-shelves of cookery books, and then there were shelves of everyday crockery.

'Tea?' offered Sheila.

'No, thank you, Miss Haggis. We have just been on a visit to Dr Farham.'

She turned round to lift the kettle onto the stove. 'So?'

'Good man for treating the drug addicts,' said Hamish.

She swung round again and looked at him defiantly. 'I'm better. Been there. Done that. I run a therapy group at Braikie hospital on Thursdays, but I bet he didn't tell you that.'

'I want to know this time,' said Hamish, 'were you perhaps *spying* on Maggie's?'

She sighed and sat down at the table and waved a small red hand to indicate they should do the same. 'I was in Inverness shopping and remembered one of the women in my group saying she had got her drugs from a grimy café on Ness Bank. I went to have a look. That's when I saw Olivia with that professor.'

'Why didn't you tell us about the drugs afore?' asked Charlie.

'I didn't know about it until last Thursday. That's why.'

81

'We'll need to take a statement from this woman.'

'I have to protect her anonymity. I will make a statement.'

'Right,' said Hamish, taking out a tape recorder, while Charlie tugged a notebook out of his pocket. 'I think we might have that tea after all. I'll take the statement back to Lochdubh and type it up and bring it back for you to sign, unless you've got a computer and printer here.'

Sheila put cups, sugar and milk, and a fat teapot on the table along with a plate of scones. 'No,' she said, 'this is dinosaur land.'

'Before we get all official,' said Hamish, 'and do try to put aside your dislike of Olivia Sinclair: you must know all the signs of drug taking. Did you notice any on Mrs Sinclair?'

She shook her head. 'But I don't believe all that rubbish about the professor being there by chance.'

Hamish recorded her statement and promised to return as soon as possible to get her to sign it.

Hamish suddenly stared at her, his eyes vacant and his mouth slightly open. What am I thinking about, wasting time talking to the village idiot? she thought with sudden impatience.

Hamish stood up abruptly. 'We've got to rush,' he said, and, followed by a startled Charlie, he sped out of the manse.

'What's up?' demanded Charlie, climbing into the passenger seat. 'I'd barely got ma teeth into one o' her scones and I had to put it back wi' the bite mark on it.'

'You should have taken it with you. Listen! We've got to find out if the prof was filmed by Strathbane Television when he was speaking. Maybe the cameras panned over the audience. I'd like to see if Olivia was there.'

Charlie shifted uncomfortably. He still saw Olivia as very attractive.

'We'd better tell Jimmy,' Hamish said. 'You phone him and tell him to meet us at the television offices.'

'Do you think we'll get through this blizzard?'

'We can try,' said Hamish. 'I think it's thinning a bit.'

By the time they reached the television offices, it was to find Jimmy pacing up and down outside. Watery sunlight was melting snow from the roofs.

'Snow,' said Hamish curtly.

'So what's this all about?' asked Jimmy.

Hamish told him and added that it might be an idea to tell Inverness to raid Maggie's for drugs. 'I have a tape recording of Sheila's statement. Once we're finished here, I'll type it up at headquarters and take it back for her to sign.'

'Why isn't our friend Blair muscling in on this?' asked Charlie.

Jimmy grinned. 'His flat went on fire. He's in hospital with burns on his fat back. Says he doesn't know how it started, but Cully, the informant, saw Blair buying an e-cigarette in the pub and it could have been one of those ones that bursts into flames when you charge them.'

'So has the wife anywhere to live?'

'Nearly didn't. The fat one hadn't paid the insurance so no temporary flat was on offer and he'll need to pay for all the repairs. So Mrs Daviot has offered them house room. What a laugh. Blair won't be able to get drunk. Okay. Let's see what we can find here.'

They were ushered from one place to another until they were finally conducted into the office of Diarmuid Lancey, who had produced the documentary on the professor. He was a big, shaggy man dressed like a lumberjack in a checked shirt and faded jeans. He had greasy black curls down to his shoulders and a black, matted beard.

'Aye, I remember the wee tosser,' he said. 'Told him after the show what a scunner he was. "You can take your lousy views and shove them up your scrawny arse," I told him.'

'You are a good Christian, Mr Lancey,' commented Hamish.

'What, me? Naw. Look, this God business comforts a lot o' folk, right? Why take it away? I dinnae go round at Christmas, grabbing hold o' bairns and saying, *There is no Santa Claus*. If you follow me to the studio, we'll run through what I've got. I got shots o' the audience in Inverness and here in Strathbane as well.'

In the studio, they leaned forward in their chairs as the camera panned over the audience. There was nothing of interest in the brief shots of the Strathbane audience, but it was when it moved to Inverness that they struck gold. There in the front row was none other than Olivia Sinclair.

Jimmy agreed that Hamish and Charlie should go back and interview her again to find out why she had said nothing about going to hear the professor speak.

On the road back, Hamish said he would leave the dogs at the police station and then they could be on their way. The snow had melted fast, and sunlight shining on the puddles of the road turned them into little lakes of molten gold. Charlie was excited at the thought of seeing Olivia again. He reminded himself that she was a married woman, but the frissons of excitement would not seem to go away.

There was an ice chest on the doorstep, with a label addressed to Charlie. 'Be careful,' cautioned Hamish. 'Could be something nasty.'

'No, it's from my cousin, Hugh. Of course, he'd think I was living here.'

Charlie carried the chest inside and set it on the table. When he opened it and examined the contents, he let out a whoop of delight.

'What is it?' asked Hamish.

'It's pickled guga, crappit heid, and carrageen pudding.'

Hamish knew that meant baby gannet, stuffed cod's head, and seaweed pudding.

85

'I warned you it might be something nasty,' said Hamish.

'You have no taste,' said Charlie huffily. 'This is a banquet for kings.'

'Never mind. We'll drop your goodies off at the castle and be on our way. Give it to Clarry to put in one of the kitchen fridges and ask him if we can bum a couple of sandwiches.'

Charlie emerged a short time later from the hotel kitchen door with a wicker hamper. 'We're in luck,' he crowed. 'One picnic hamper left over.'

They stopped by a burn before they reached Olivia's home. The hamper contained not only sandwiches but a thermos of coffee. They ate and drank contentedly until Hamish said, 'I might have an idea to get to her before her husband comes home.'

'Oh, aye,' said Charlie. 'I keep forgetting about him.'

Hamish looked at him sharply. 'Not keen on her, are you?'

'Me. No!' And Charlie crossed his fingers behind his back. People never think of policemen as dreamers, but if they did not have some sort of fantasy life to counteract the horrors of their job they might go bonkers.

So it was that Charlie remembered the glorious feast and suddenly saw himself entertaining Olivia to dinner.

His dream nearly died when Olivia did not look particularly pleased to see them. She was even less pleased when Hamish explained the reason for their visit.

'I didn't think it important. There's nothing much else to do up here but go and watch a freak show.'

'But when he – as you said – approached you in Maggie's, you told us nothing about having already seen him.'

'All right!' she shouted, clutching her hair. 'I'd talked to him after the show. He was awfully boring. That's all. I was ashamed of having been to a gig like that. I mean, I don't give a monkey's tail about God, one way or the other.'

'Did you know that there's a good possibility of drugs being sold at Maggie's?'

'No, I did not. Enough. I am not answering any more questions without my lawyer.'

Outside Hamish said, 'Got that on the recorder?'

'I've left it behind!'

Charlie rushed back into the house in time to see Olivia picking up the small tape recorder. 'I'll take that,' he said, seizing it.

She suddenly fell into his arms and burst into tears. 'I'm frightened of my husband finding out I went to that lecture,' she sobbed. 'Why do you think he leaves me stuck out here? He's madly possessive.'

One thin white hand with long red nails clutched at his regulation sweater. 'I shouldn't have said that about a lawyer, should I?'

'Well … no,' said Charlie awkwardly. 'Makes you look guilty. Why don't we talk it over, say, this evening?

Come to my wee place at the castle for dinner, you and your husband.'

Her tears dried as if by magic. It was like watching a film played backwards.

'You are so good,' she breathed. 'What time?'

'Eight o'clock.'

'We'll be there.'

Charlie decided not to tell Hamish about his invitation. Hamish would lecture him. But he had invited the husband as well so all was correct. Charlie did not like the way Hamish had jeered at the delicacies of the Hebrides. On the road back, he sat wrapped in a happy dream of how Olivia's beautiful eyes would widen when she saw the banquet.

That evening, Charlie was glad that the colonel and his wife were off visiting friends because he was sure George would have tried to butt in.

He was so happy in his little home that he rarely broke anything. A peat fire warmed the living room. The table was laid with a white cloth pinched from the dining room. A bottle of Chablis was chilling in an ice bucket in the pantry. The room was lit by one standard lamp casting a golden glow on the crystal glasses on the table.

Charlie had brushed his fair hair until it shone. He was wearing a blue linen shirt over dark-blue cords.

Exactly at eight o'clock, he heard footsteps descending the stone stairs to his basement.

Olivia entered. She was alone.

'Where is Mr Sinclair?' asked Charlie.

'Oh, he had work to do. Help me off with my coat.'

Olivia was wearing a mink coat. When Charlie removed it, he saw she had on a skimpy little black dress with a plunging neckline and a very short skirt.

'We should be chaperoned,' said Charlie.

'Oh, you adorable bear. I'm not going to *seduce* you.'

Charlie blushed and shuffled his feet. But he could not bear to give up sharing the glory of these delicacies.

'Take a seat,' he said. He brought the wine and poured two glasses. Then he said, 'Now, this is a real Hebridean delicacy.'

He went out to what had been the old butler's pantry and came back with plates containing slices of pickled guga and salad.

Olivia took a first mouthful. It was, she thought, like chewing salted rubber.

'What on earth is this?' she demanded.

'It's guga,' said Charlie proudly. 'And you'll never guess what's to follow.'

'What?'

'Crappit heid.'

'Do you mean to say there is actually a dish which sounds as if it is a head that someone has crapped in?'

'It is the cod's head stuffed wi' oatmeal,' said Charlie desperately. 'And there's carrageen pudding for afters.'

Olivia rose to her feet, knocking her chair backwards in her haste. 'You're quite right. I shouldn't have come. Help me on with my coat. Oh, don't just stand there with your mouth open.'

Silently he helped her into her coat and followed her upstairs. In the reception area Olivia turned and faced him. 'Did you really expect me to eat that peasant muck?'

And Charlie, regrettably, lost his temper. 'Shove off afore I strangle ye, ye rotten bitch!' he yelled.

The manager, Mr Johnson, came out of his office; people spilled out of the bar as Olivia stalked out to her car.

'Into my office, Charlie,' ordered Mr Johnson. He ushered Charlie in and shut the door. 'Now, what are you doing creating a scene like that?'

Charlie hung his head and blurted out the whole story while the manager tried not to laugh.

At last, Mr Johnson said, 'Just don't ever throw a scene like that again.'

'Isn't there anyone from the islands on the staff that might like a bit?'

'Not unless they eat things like that in Poland. And anyone in Lochdubh will have eaten the evening meal around six o'clock. It's still high tea in Lochdubh. There's old Lady Crannock in the dining room. She's from Uist.'

Charlie shot out before Mr Johnson could stop him. By the time he had chased Charlie into the dining room, the tall policeman was bending over Lady Crannock and talking rapidly.

'Go away, Charlie,' said Mr Johnson. 'My lady, I must apologize . . .'

'Out of my way. This young man is taking me to dinner.' Lady Crannock put one old gnarled hand on Charlie's arm and together they walked out of the dining room.

Charlie's dinner was a success at last. Lady Crannock ate every bit of guga, declared the crappit heid 'divine', and entertained Charlie with tales of South Uist in the old days. She said that she came to the hotel every year 'to be looked after'.

How old was she? Charlie wondered. Her face was brown and covered in a criss-cross of wrinkles. Her small black eyes were bright with intelligence. But he realized, when she had finished most of the wine, there was not often such a thing as a sweet old lady as he removed her heavily ringed hand from his knee for the fourth time.

When he had finally escorted her upstairs and said good night, he found his conscience was hurting him. Hamish would no doubt hear about the scene with Olivia. How could he have been so stupid?

He could not begin to imagine the horror that was to descend on him.

Chapter Five

Marriage is like life in this – that it is a field of battle, and not a bed of roses.
—Robert Louis Stevenson

Ailsa, Jock's red-haired wife, was stacking up crates of empty bottles at the back of the store. She stopped her work to admire a pair of buzzards sailing up against a clear blue sky and wondered if they might be in for a spell of good weather at last.

She saw villager Edie Aubrey and waved to her. 'You'll never believe it,' panted Edie, running up to join Ailsa.

'Believe what?' asked Ailsa, thinking that Edie was a bit like an eager dog, her brown eyes gleaming under a heavy fringe.

'Jimmy Lauchlan, him what helps out in the kitchen at the Tommel Castle, well, he says there was such a stramash there last night. It was thon big loon of a copper, Charlie something, and Olivia Sinclair.'

'Go on.'

'They came up from the basement and he shouts he's going to kill her!'

'My, my. I wish he *would* kill the bitch. Last time she came in the shop and spoke to Jock, she leaned over the counter and her neckline was so low he could see her tits. And she's got the minister not knowing whether he's coming or going.'

'The ghosts have gone quiet anyway,' said Edie. 'Must have been smuggler folk.'

'They can't have come up the loch,' said Ailsa. 'I mean folk would have heard a boat. Oh, talking of Olivia, isn't that madam over there?'

'Where?'

'Up by the castle, sitting on that rock. She's bent over, looking at something on the ground, but I recognize that mink coat. Like a coffee? Jock's caved in and bought one of the new machines.'

'Aye, that would be grand.'

'It's too fine a day to go inside. Sit down on a crate and I'll bring it out to you. It's milk and two sugars?'

'Aye.'

Edie turned her face up to the sun. Somehow, despite the murder of the professor, fear had left Drim. Smugglers were of this earth, not like ghosts.

Ailsa soon returned and handed her a mug of coffee. 'Try that, Edie. Better than that instant muck. I was just saying to Jock the other day . . . Look at that! She's still crouched over.'

'Olivia?'

'Aye, herself. Oh, dammit to hell. I'd better go and make sure she isn't ill.'

As Ailsa approached the still figure, she had a sudden feeling of dread. It was early in the morning and Olivia's coat sparkled with dew.

'Olivia,' she shouted. She put a hand on her shoulder. No reaction.

Ailsa walked round the rock and peered up into Olivia's face. That face was clay white. 'You are ill. Come on. Up you get.' She slid her strong arms inside Olivia's coat and tried to lift her. That was when Olivia's head tilted back and Ailsa saw the cruel red marks on her neck.

She ran back, shouting to Edie. 'She's dead. Murdered. Dead. Don't just stand there. *Dead, dead, dead!*'

Hamish received the news just after Charlie had joined him in the police station. 'I'll phone Jimmy,' said Hamish. 'I suppose we are the ones who'll have to break the news to the husband. Why, Charlie! Man, you're as white as a sheet!'

'I was with her yesterday evening,' said Charlie.

'You what? Why?'

'It was the guga and stuff. I told her about it when I went back for the tape recorder. On impulse, I invited her and her husband tae dinner. She turned up alone.'

'I can see from your face, Charlie, that there's worse to come. Out wi' it.'

'She sneered at the food and stomped out. In reception, she called it peasant muck and I felt she was insulting my whole heritage. I shouted at her. I threatened to strangle her. Mr Johnson heard me and some of the guests as well.'

'She *was* strangled, Charlie. What happened after that?'

'There was this auld biddie, Lady Crannock from Uist, and I invited her and she loved every bit o' it.'

'So that takes us up to what time?'

'About eleven thirty.'

'So let's hope forensics find she was killed afore then. But police headquarters are going to find out about you living at the hotel unless we can stop it. Now, your friend, Colonel Halburton-Smythe, is always anxious to play the great detective. Get on the phone and ask him to help you with an excuse.'

While Charlie went outside to phone, Hamish called Jimmy and told him all about Olivia's visit to the hotel and how Charlie had been heard threatening her. Hamish ended up by saying, 'You know Charlie's got a wee flat at the hotel. Try to keep that quiet.' Hamish could hear Jimmy roaring with laughter. 'What's so bloody funny?'

'I was just thinking,' gasped Jimmy, 'of a sophisticated bitch like Olivia Sinclair, star of hunt balls and other snobby events, being faced with a pickled seagull.'

'Will you tell the husband or shall I?' demanded Hamish.

'You do it. Tell Charlie he's off the case and to sit tight. I would tell you to leave it to Tain police but I'd like you to size up his reaction. We're Police Scotland and just the one big happy family. So if anyone over there objects, tell them that.'

Hamish rang off just as Charlie came back in. 'You're suspended, Charlie. But we'll get you off the hook as soon as possible.'

'Is it all right if I go to see George? He's sure he can fix things.'

'Well, I hope the colonel can do something. Off with you, and look after the dogs.'

Hamish drove out, noticing the weather had turned colder. The remains of the snow had frozen into surrealist bars across the moors. A sign that the day was to remain dry and fine lay in the mountains, which appeared to have taken a step backwards. When rain was coming, they appeared to crowd closer, every crevice and gully in sharp relief as on a steel engraving.

He sighed. Olivia must have been trying to fascinate Charlie so that he would tell her everything about the case. Why? What had she to hide? Hamish had judged her to be highly manipulative. And what had she been doing on a rock near the castle? Ailsa had said there was dew on her coat. That would mean she had been there early in the morning. No, wait a bit. If it turned colder, then dew, which was just condensation, could form during the night. So say, she had phoned someone from her car after leaving Charlie and that someone had suggested a meet in Drim. The road to Tain took him past the Sinclairs' home. He had just left it behind when he saw a Range Rover speeding in the opposite direction with Selwyn Sinclair at the wheel. Hamish did a U-turn and put on the siren and the blue light. In front of him, Selwyn screeched to a halt.

Hamish got down from the Land Rover and Selwyn, in front of him, got out of his car.

'I'm right sorry, sir,' began Hamish.

'Well, I'm sorry I was speeding, Officer. Can't we let it go this time?'

Hamish, who had assumed the grieving husband had heard the news of his wife's murder and was heading for either home or Drim, realized he had not yet learned of her death.

Removing his cap and tucking it under his arm, Hamish said, 'I am afraid I have bad news for you, sir.'

'What bad news?'

'Your wife was murdered, maybe last night, sir. Her body was found at Drim.'

Selwyn's reaction startled Hamish. 'Stupid bitch,' said Selwyn. 'What the hell was she up to this time?'

'Perhaps,' suggested Hamish soothingly, 'we could go to your house and you can tell me, as you did not know about your wife's death, what you were doing racing home?'

Selwyn gave a curt nod and walked back to his car.

Uncomfortable house, thought Hamish, as he waited for Selwyn to get out of his outdoor clothes. You'd think the photographers from *House & Garden* would be arriving any moment. Bet you it was done by an interior decorator. He was puzzled by Selwyn's behaviour. Surely a man who had just been told his wife had been murdered wouldn't delay by changing out of his outdoor clothes.

He finally reappeared with a dry martini in one hand and a cigarette in the other. He had taken off not only his coat but his business suit as well and was wearing jeans and a sweater.

He had one of those smooth gin-and-sauna faces with a large curved nose over a small mouth. His fair hair was brushed flat against his skull, and his eyes were dark grey.

'Sit down,' he ordered. 'Now, out with it.'

'Your wife, Olivia Sinclair, was found in Drim this morning. She had been strangled. At first estimate, it looks as if she might have been killed during the night. Where were you last night, sir?'

'I was here. In bed.'

'And did you see your wife at any time?'

'No, we have separate bedrooms. I did not check hers. I had a long day's work and went straight to bed. I had dinner with some Japanese businessmen at the Caledonian in Inverness and did not get back here until after midnight. I stopped outside Inverness for petrol and I have the receipt. Also the bill for the dinner.'

'Why would your wife have gone to Drim? We're not yet sure of the time of death. But why would she go there in any case?'

'To screw up someone's life, I assume. What a damn mistake I made getting married to her.'

Hamish could hear the sound of approaching sirens. Jimmy would not butt in but Blair would.

'I think that is my superior officer,' said Hamish.

To Selwyn's surprise, Hamish disappeared into the back of the house just as there came a hammering at the front door.

Selwyn opened it to find himself confronted by Detective Chief Inspector Blair, his hairy hands still bandaged up. He was accompanied by a female detective and a police sergeant.

'Mr Selwyn Sinclair,' said Blair. 'You are to accompany us to police headquarters in Strathbane for questioning.'

'I'm going for a pee first,' said Selwyn. Once in the bathroom, he phoned Superintendent Daviot. 'What the hell is this man Blair doing, Peter?' he raged. 'My wife has just been murdered and the fool is trying to drag me off in handcuffs.'

'Put him on the phone, now,' said Daviot. 'This is dreadful.'

Selwyn emerged from the bathroom to find Blair standing outside. 'Superintendent Daviot wants a word with you,' he said.

Blair gingerly took the proffered mobile. The phone clacked busily. Blair finally handed it back to Selwyn, his face scarlet.

'I hope you've told the fool to take a run and jump,' Blair heard Selwyn say. 'Before he turned up, I was being correctly and professionally interviewed by a copper named Macbeth. If you want more out of me, get him back.'

As he drove off, Blair cursed and fumed. Somehow, he would prove Selwyn Sinclair guilty of murder, and he was prepared to bribe for information and fake evidence if that's what it took.

Hamish's radio sprang into life with the voice of Daviot ordering him to take over the questioning of Selwyn.

Once again, as he drove back, Hamish marvelled at the way Blair kept his job. But he always crawled to Daviot. No one else did, apart from secretary Helen. And Daviot was fundamentally a weak man. Still, if Blair found out about Charlie staying at the castle, he would have ammunition.

Daviot was pleasantly surprised to receive a phone call from Colonel Halburton-Smythe. 'I was wondering,' said the colonel, 'if you and Mrs Daviot would care to be my guests for dinner tonight? I have a little problem and I would be glad of your advice.'

'We are delighted to accept,' said Daviot. 'What time?'

'Say, eight o'clock?' said the colonel.

'Splendid. I will do all I can to help you with your problem.'

After he had rung off, Daviot phoned his wife to tell

her about the dinner invitation. 'Oh, what'll I wear?' she shrieked. 'I'll need to buy a new gown.'

'Oh, do what you want,' said the super expansively. To Daviot and his friends at the lodge, Tommel Castle Hotel was the equivalent of Claridge's in London, and the Halburton-Smythes were considered the local aristocracy. Perhaps their friends Lord and Lady Caithness might be there.

So Blair was lucky when he crept in later to fulsomely apologize and was merely told that his burns must still be hurting and affecting his judgement and to take two days off.

Back in Selwyn's living room, Hamish said cautiously, 'You do not seem particularly distressed about the death of your wife.'

'No, I am not. It'll spare me the expense of the divorce she was trying not to give me.'

'So who is the next Mrs Sinclair going to be?'

'What on earth gave you that stupid idea?' yelled Selwyn. 'I've had enough of bloody women.'

'I do apologize,' said Hamish meekly. 'It's just that love for someone else often prompts a divorce. May I ask, sir, why you obviously did not like her? You see, the more I know about her, the better chance I have of understanding her character. If I feel I know the person, it helps me find out who might have murdered them.'

'I see what you're after. Well, Olivia was one chief manipulator. She liked finding out about people so she could make them twist and turn in her claws. Small example: I had a pretty secretary three months ago. She got drunk at a hen party and did a bit of a striptease, not the lot, just stood on a table and waved her knickers in the air. Somehow, Olivia was there and videoed the whole thing and put it out on social media. That poor girl not only fled from the job but from the Highlands as well. Why did I marry Olivia in the first place?

'She promised so many delights of sex and yet was so clever about it that the first time I really had her was on our honeymoon. It was like shagging a corpse. I suppose I'd better identify the body.'

'Did Mrs Sinclair not have any family?'

'No, she was an only child. If she had any relatives, I never heard of them. A friend of hers acted as brides-maid. What was her name? Droopy creature. Bethany Pollock, that's it! I'll have the address somewhere. Lives in Perth.'

Hamish phoned ahead to make sure that the body had been moved to the mortuary in Strathbane. Selwyn said he would use his own car and so they met outside the mortuary and walked in together.

After Selwyn had identified the body of his wife, Hamish stayed behind and said to the mortuary technician, 'If you've got the professor here, may I have a look at him?'

'Sure, mac. Got him ower here. Still on the slab. His sister, Miss Alice Gordon, is due any minute.'

'What's the official cause of death?'

'Broken neck, maybe. But with him being bashed around the sea and the little fishies dining off the soft parts, it's hard to tell. Tried to put the sister off but she would insist on coming.' He tilted his head to one side. Hamish noticed he had very small, very pointed ears. The old people would damn him as a changeling: that is, when the fairies snatch a baby and leave one of their own in its place. 'I bet that's her now.'

The door opened and a policewoman entered with a small, thickset woman wearing an old-fashioned musquash coat with large furry buttons. She was wearing a matching fur hat pulled down low on her forehead. Her eyes were small and brown. She looked like an outraged animal, disturbed during hibernation.

'Where is my brother?' she demanded. The technician indicated a slab on the right and gently rolled back the sheet from the face.

'That is he,' she declared majestically. 'I wish him to be cremated. He didn't believe in hellfire, but just in case it is real, it might be nice to give him a foretaste.' And with that, she burst out laughing. When she finally stopped, Hamish said, 'I will take you to the procurator fiscal's office so they may tell you when the body is to be released.'

When he had finally finished with her, he went to police headquarters to type up his report on Selwyn Sinclair. Jimmy Anderson came and leaned over his shoulder.

'Anything?'

Hamish looked round at him. 'If you die, Jimmy, I should be right sorry.'

'This is so sudden, old fruit. What brought this on?'

Hamish told him about Selwyn's hatred for his wife and about the professor's sister, howling with laugher.

'I've got three ex-wives who'd probably dance on my grave,' said Jimmy. 'Cheer up, Hamish. I've got a sister who loves me.'

Suddenly Blair followed by Daviot erupted into the room. 'We've got them,' shouted Daviot. 'The smugglers. They were wrecked off the west coast and the coast-guard got them with a cargo of cigarettes. Real ones. And one of them's got plans of that room under the tower and the passage. Murders solved!'

As Daviot triumphantly crowed over the arrest, Hamish felt uneasy. Vicious drug smugglers, he could under-stand. But was trade in contraband cigarettes enough to kill two people?

'Who are they?' Jimmy demanded.

'They're a gang o' teenagers from Glasgow who call themselves the Springburn Boys. Ringleader is one Creepy Jesus, real name, John Torrance.'

'So what's with the Creepy Jesus name?' asked Jimmy.

'Found God when he was once in a young offenders' institution. Got the nickname there and it stuck.'

'How many in this gang?' asked Hamish.

'Five.'

'And which one is the expert skipper?'

'Turns out, according to the coastguard, they didn't know one end of a boat from the other. Stole the boat in Strathbane, seen sailing erratically, and then got too near the cliffs and the boat began to smash up. Coastguard had to call in air-sea rescue because they couldn't get close enough to lift them off.'

'And they've confessed to the murders?'

'Really, Macbeth,' said Daviot, 'you are slowing up everything with all these questions. Get back to your beat.'

Jimmy followed Hamish out. 'You should be glad o' the news. Lets your chum off the hook.'

'I wish I could be in on the interviews,' said Hamish. 'Look! If you've got five of them all saying yes to smuggling and no to murder, you won't have much to take to court. And a sympathetic jury will let them off on the smuggling charge. I mean, cigarettes! If I were their lawyer, I'd be searching for smokers on the jury.'

'I don't get it,' said Jimmy. 'You like lazing around the village and avoiding promotion. So what's the big, fat hairy deal? Case solved.'

'I don't think it is,' said Hamish stubbornly.

'Well, if you find anything, my bonny heiland laddie, don't tell me. I'm off to the pub.'

* * *

Hamish drove slowly back to Lochdubh, his mind racing. Two murders on his beat! And he was sure the young smugglers had nothing to do with it. When he got to the station, he phoned Charlie with the news, ending with, 'I'm sure the murderer is still out there. But it lets you off the hook for the time being.'

'Should I cancel that dinner? George has invited the Daviots.'

'No, let them come. Daviot'll be so impressed that he won't want to hear anything against you. But don't go to the dinner yourself. Daviot's a snob. Come here instead and bring the dogs. I'll make supper.'

Hamish looked at the phone after he had rung off, trying to remember if he knew anyone sympathetic in Glasgow. Then he remembered Rowan Southey. He hailed originally from the Black Isle and knew Hamish and some of the Macbeth family.

He looked up a battered old notebook, full of addresses and numbers he had kept meaning to transfer to his iPad and never got around to. He tried Strathclyde police but was told Rowan was off ill. He phoned his home number and Rowan himself answered the phone. After he had reintroduced himself, Hamish said, 'You're on sick leave? What's up with you?'

'Aye, it's a bad terminal illness called Police Scotland. Had to get off to go to an interview in London. Big security firm. Bodyguard job. Big money. Took it. Can't wait until the morrow when I can tell them where to put their forms and targets and you name it right up their—'

'I get the picture. Could you find out something afore you go?' asked Hamish.

'What?'

'We've just arrested a gang o' smugglers for murder. Led by a cheil called Creepy Jesus.'

'Aw, pull the ither one, mac. Creepy Jesus is all wind and piss. He couldnae say boo tae a goose.'

'What's he usually been done for?'

'Petty theft. Drunk and disorderly. Peddling cigarettes. Nobody bothered about the cigs. I mean, gangs go out to wherever in the world is the cheapest and bring them back by the truckload. Then they hand them out to the lesser gangs to sell to the shops and a few cartons to people like Creepy to push in pubs. Mind you, they've catching a lot of the trucks now. Heard they was coming in by boat. So maybe Creepy, who'd always got big ideas offa the fillums, decided to cut out the middlemen and go get the fags himself.

'I'm telling you, Hamish, those lads are safer off in jail 'cos the big boys were bringing drugs as well. Someone tried to pocket a bit o' money for themselves and you dinnae want tae hear what happened to him afore they threw the carcase in the Clyde.'

Hamish thanked him and rang off. He was about to switch on the computer and type up Selwyn's statement as Strathbane would like it, all angles covered, although nothing would make them change their minds, when he decided the best thing he could do was forget about the whole thing for one evening.

Hamish changed out of his uniform into comfortable shabby clothes and walked along to Patel's grocery store. God bless the Asians, he thought, not for the first time. Mr Patel now seemed to stock everything anyone could want and had opened up a butcher's counter to sell local meat and fish.

Hamish decided a big fry-up would suit them both and bought haggis, venison sausages, eggs, bacon, mushrooms, tomatoes, and two slices of dumpling.

Charlie arrived an hour later to find Hamish standing turning things in an enormous frying pan.

Soon, they sat down to an enormous supper, washed down with beer. 'I hope George is enjoying his dinner as much as I'm loving this,' said Charlie.

But later that evening, George, Colonel Halburton-Smythe, was beginning to become seriously alarmed. For he had praised Charlie so much that finally Daviot, warmed with fine food, wine, and snobbery, said expansively, 'It's time he was promoted. I'll move him straight to Strathbane.'

The colonel thought so hard, he could feel a headache coming on. 'Peter,' he said at last. 'May I call you Peter?'

'Of course,' said Daviot, beaming with gratification.

'It's like this. I must swear you both to secrecy.'

'Certainly,' both breathed in unison.

'Charlie is the illegitimate son of the Kerensey family.'

'You mean Lord Kerensey?' asked Mrs Daviot, eyes goggling.

'Shhh!' implored the colonel. 'He was given to a Mrs Carter out in Uist to bring up as her own. That is why I allow Charlie a wee apartment here to look after him. He's too big for the police station and he's young. So he is better here in Lochdubh where I can keep an eye on him. But this secret is to be kept just between us.'

The Daviots were flooded with gratification and the colonel, who knew his wife was due back late that evening, hoped to get rid of the Daviots before she arrived.

When his visitors had gone, the little colonel scampered down the stairs to tell Charlie the good news. Charlie was just about to go to bed, but he listened eagerly as George explained that there would be no trouble about his staying at the castle from that day on.

Charlie heard him out and then said bitterly, 'So I'm supposed to thank you for calling me a bastard. My poor mither would turn in her grave if she could have heard you. You can keep your damn flat. I'm off to the station.'

It showed how desperate the colonel was when he cried, 'Get Hamish here. He'll understand.'

And Charlie, who felt that George deserved a real lecture, phoned Hamish and asked him to come as quickly as he could.

They sat in silence, on either side of the fire. George was frightened of losing the only real friend he had ever had. His father had made a lot of money out of shoe shops and so young George had been sent to public school and then Sandhurst Military Academy, where he had adopted a sort of military stage persona to cover his fears of not fitting in.

Hamish arrived and listened to the colonel's tale of his lies to the Daviots and tried very hard not to laugh.

When the colonel had finished, Hamish said, 'But why such an elaborate story?'

'It was when I realized I had praised Charlie too much that Daviot said he would move him to Strathbane.'

'You didnae tell me that bit,' said Charlie.

'I was concentrating so hard on finding a way to let you stay on in this flat.'

'Look,' said Hamish, 'leave it to me. I know how to restore your honour, Charlie, and get you off the hook, Colonel.'

'How?' they both chorused.

Hamish grinned. 'Listen and learn.'

He dialled Daviot's home number. Daviot was still awake having a nightcap with his wife while they mulled over the success of the evening.

'You'd better have a good excuse for phoning this number, Macbeth,' said Daviot.

Hamish's voice took on the crooning highland lilt it always adopted when he was about to tell one whopping lie.

'It is like this, sir. Colonel Halburton-Smythe told you that Charlie Carter was illegitimate.'

'In confidence, may I remind you!'

110

'But that is not true and the colonel is upset. He was frightened of losing Charlie to Strathbane and he so valued your acquaintance that he made up the first thing that came into his head. You see, Carter is too big to fit into the police station and a posh hotel like Tommel Castle is always being plagued with petty thieves and such. So if you don't mind Charlie staying on, the colonel is anxious to apologize to you in person and his wife is anxious to meet you. He suggests another evening, say, next Wednesday?'

And Daviot, who had just begun think that Hamish was making a fool of him as usual, forgot his suspicions at the sound of Mrs Halburton-Smythe's name, for the Halburtons were aristocracy. Perhaps the colonel's wife could put a word in for him at the palace. Sir Peter Daviot. He could hear it. He could feel the royal sword on his shoulder.

'Sir?' demanded Hamish, wondering if the line had gone dead.

'What? Oh, yes, my wife and I will be delighted to attend. Carter can stay.'

But it all nearly came unstuck the following day. Daviot wanted to brag, and who better to brag to than Detective Chief Inspector Blair.

Blair acted duly impressed, shaking his head in well-manufactured wonder and saying, 'My, it's the palace for you next. Mind you, it would be right awful if Carter had been charging relocation money. I mean, he's only

111

supposed to do that if we relocate him, otherwise he might have been claiming eight thousand pounds for just going along the road, after having claimed relocation expenses to Lochdubh.'

Daviot summoned Helen. 'You may go, Blair,' he snapped.

'I was only trying to help,' said Blair, edging crabwise to the door.

'In your usual way,' said Daviot bitterly. When Blair had gone, he instructed Helen to find out about Charles Carter's expenses.

Blair did not know it, but Daviot had started for the first time to think up ways of getting rid of him. For Daviot could not even bask in the glory of solved murders for worry that Carter had been cheating and that his precious dinner would go up in smoke.

His heart sank when Helen bustled in late that afternoon saying, 'I am afraid there is a problem with Constable Carter's expenses.'

'What is it?'

'When he was transferred to Lochdubh, he forgot to claim any money for relocation.'

The sun shone on the landscape of Daviot's mind once more. 'Inform the man to claim for the removal, Helen. Anything nice for tea?'

'I've got empire biscuits.'

'Wonderful!' Soon Daviot was crunching on two layers of biscuit with jam in the middle, and icing and a cherry on top.

He glared as Blair walked in unannounced. 'What is it?'

'I was just wondering about that . . .'

'If you mean Carter's relocation expenses, he didn't claim anything at all.'

'Och, that is good news. My! Would that be an empire biscuit?'

Daviot heard Helen arriving back outside. He rang the buzzer. 'Mr Blair is leaving,' he said icily.

'Aye, aye.' Blair shuffled his feet. 'See you at the lodge this evening?'

But Daviot, his eyes once more full of dreams and his mouth full of biscuit, did not deign to reply.

Chapter Six

Man is the only one to whom the torture and death
of his fellow creatures is amusing in itself.
                                   —James Anthony Froude

The next morning, Hamish felt spring had really arrived at last. A warm frisky wind blew in from the west. As he strolled along the waterfront, his dogs at his heels, he longed to put his doubts to one side, forget about wrong people being accused of murder, and return to the lazy life he loved so much.

He was accosted by the minister's wife. Mrs Wellington never went out of doors without a hat. The latest number was like an Indiana Jones special except that the hatband was decorated with a sprig of fake heather.

'I was looking at the ages of those murderers in the morning newspaper,' she said. 'All so young! What a waste of young lives.' She was joined by the Currie sisters, uniformly dressed in camel-hair coats.

'Aye,' said Nessie. 'But it's a good thing we have the

coastguard, because if it was left to this loon here, we wouldn't be safe in our beds.'

'Safe in our beds,' echoed the Greek chorus that was her sister.

Hamish hardly ever lost his temper, but all his worry about the case came up to the surface and he shouted, 'Oh, shove off!' He strode off along the waterfront with his dogs scampering at his heels.

'I know just what to do about him!' said Mrs Wellington.

'Pray for him?' asked Nessie, echoed by her sister.

'No. That one needs a good strong woman to sort him out. I'll get my niece, Heather Lomond, to come on a wee visit. I'll have them married as soon as possible. She'll soon sort him out.'

'He likes them pretty,' warned Nessie.

'Handsome is as handsome does,' said Mrs Wellington, who appeared to have a bottomless fund of clichés.

Hamish saw Charlie strolling towards him, the policeman having decided to walk down from the castle. Hamish explained why he had just been rude to the Currie sisters and Mrs Wellington.

'Aye, it bothers me as well,' said Charlie. 'A good lawyer could get them off. I mean, no one's found a murder weapon. They admitted using the tower basement to stock the stuff. Before, they had an expert skipper belonging to the Glasgow gang, them that set up the machinery to produce the wails and noises. Then the wee lads thought they'd cut out the middleman.'

'I meant to ask,' said Hamish. 'I assume they found the machinery responsible for the hauntings?'

'Yes, hidden up on top of the old tower and set on a timer. It was very cleverly concealed amongst the ivy, which is why they didn't find it first time.'

'Let's go back to the station and go over the notes,' said Hamish.

It was only when he was seated at his desk in the office that Hamish realized his folly in letting Charlie make coffee. The sound of breaking china sent him rushing to the kitchen. Red with mortification, Charlie was staring down miserably at two shattered coffee cups. Hamish looked at the broken shards and realized they were two cups bought by Christine that he had loathed. One bore the legend CHAUVINIST PIG and the other, WOMEN OF THE WORLD UNITE.

'It's all right,' said Hamish soothingly. 'Go into the living room and sit down with the dogs and watch something on TV.'

'I'll replace them,' said Charlie.

'Don't you dare. Off you go.'

Hamish made coffee and poured some into another cup, also a relic of Christine. It bore the legend MEN ARE GOOD FOR NOTHING. He carried it in to Charlie.

'That's real decent of you,' said Charlie with an

expansive wave of his arm which sent cup and contents flying on to the hearth, where the cup shattered.

Charlie leapt to his feet and banged his head on the ceiling and sank back on the sofa with a groan.

'I've got a grand idea,' said Hamish. 'You go out and take the dogs and all of you get into the Land Rover. We'll drive up to the hotel and pay Clarry to make us up coffee and sandwiches and then go somewhere quiet to sit and talk about the case. Off you go!'

Hamish drove up to the Falls of Anstey. He was surprised to see that the recently derelict gift shop was now open again. It turned out to be owned and run by a Polish couple.

'Immigrants everywhere,' grumbled Charlie as they sat on a flat rock above the falls.

'And thank goodness for that,' said Hamish. 'Where would the Highlands be without them? That gift shop has been closed for ages. No one else wanted to have it. Now, when we've finished eating, let's have a hard think about the murders.'

The sun sparkled on the racing water. A balmy breeze blew in from the west. Fresh green leaves shivered on a stand of birch trees. When they had finished, Hamish raised his voice above the noise of the falls and said, 'We'd better find somewhere quieter.'

They went back to where they had left the Land Rover in the gift shop car park, Hamish planning to have coffee at one of the tables outside, but a tour bus had just driven up.

They got into the police car and headed further up on to the moors. 'That's George's land over on the right. Oh, look! There's George fishing. It's a rare day for the fishing, Hamish.'

Hamish stopped the car. 'You're no good to me today. Off you go.'

'Thanks. I'll get some trout for your dinner.'

Hamish watched Charlie scamper off like a large schoolboy let out of school. He remembered wistfully the days when he could discuss cases with Priscilla. But there was no woman in his life now to listen to him. He did not know that, at that very moment, the minister's wife was planning to change that.

'So, Heather,' Mrs Wellington was booming into an old-fashioned black phone. 'You've been a widow long enough. In this village, the local policeman needs someone to sort his life out, so why don't you come on a wee visit and see what you can do.'

Once back at the station, Hamish remembered his friend, the doctor's wife, Angela Brodie. She had been of help to him in the past. He told the dogs to stay and took himself off along the waterfront to Angela's cottage. It was the only cottage with its back to the loch. It was a modern, ugly grey building, built in the 1940s to house the first doctor in the village. It fronted on to the road. You entered through a strip of garden at the back. Hamish called it a crofter's garden because it was full of bits of discarded machinery, witness to Angela's failed trials of electronic baking equipment from blenders to bread makers.

In answer to his knock, Angela called, 'Come in.' Hamish walked into her messy kitchen. As usual, Angela was seated at the end of the cluttered kitchen table, scowling at a computer screen.

'How's the latest detective story going?' asked Hamish.

'I've stopped writing them.'

'Why?'

'Can't compete with bestsellers like Stuart MacBride, so why even try? I don't have his talent. I was talked into writing them. My forte is writing stuff damned as literary which gets prizes but little money. Anyway, sit down. I'm glad of a break.'

Hamish smiled at her. Angela had a rather vague face and wispy hair, her cooking was awful, and she was a rotten housekeeper, and yet Hamish thought the doctor was lucky to have such a great wife. Angela would no more consider managing anyone's life than she would consider jumping off a cliff. She was kind and caring and the best listener in Lochdubh. Angela surprised him by pouring a slug of malt whisky into his coffee.

'I hear Mrs Wellington's about to get you married,' said Angela.

'Is that the reason for the whisky?'

'Thought you would need a bracer. I met the Currie sisters and they told me that Mrs Wellington has a niece who needs a husband and you need the love of a good woman to reform you. Got any holiday owing?'

'Maybe she's pretty,' said Hamish. 'But maybe she's got a tweedy soul. I want to talk to you about these murders.'

'Supposed to be solved. So begin at the beginning and go on to the end.'

Hamish talked and talked. The whisky sank lower in the bottle as Angela kept refilling their mugs without bothering about any more coffee.

When he had finished, Angela said, 'I think Daviot's gone mad. There is no concrete evidence to tie these young lads to the murder.'

'Aye, but it's been through the sheriff's court and heading for the High Court in Edinburgh. They seem to think the circumstantial evidence is enough.'

'Let me think,' said Angela. 'I know. I've got an idea. Have you heard of Ruby Souter?'

'No.'

'She was at school with me. I've got her phone number somewhere. She's a ball-breaking advocate and publicity-mad. And a feminist. Now, if I ask her to take on this case for the defence, she might if she thinks she'd get a lot of headlines. That's the first thing. Then I've heard a lot about Professor Gordon. This is still John Knox country and his anti-God, anti-Jesus rants roused hatred in a lot of bosoms.'

'And Olivia was a manipulator!' exclaimed Hamish.

'What if she knew something about the professor's murder?'

'There'sh another thing you sheem to be avoiding,' said Angela. Her eyes began to close.

'No, don't go to sleep,' said Hamish, realizing the whisky had suddenly made Angela drunk.

'Friend at the cashel. Him. Where did money come from?' And with that, Angela gently laid her head on the kitchen table and went to sleep.

I've never seen Angela drunk before, thought Hamish wildly. He went into the living room and fetched a cushion and slid it under her head.

As he walked to the police station and the fresh air hit him, he began to feel drunk himself. He began to do cartwheels along the waterfront. Nessie Currie let the net curtain fall back into place and phoned Mrs Wellington to tell her that Macbeth had taken to the bottle.

Two days later, Hamish was preparing a leisurely breakfast when there came a loud knocking at the front door. He went through to the living room and shouted, 'Side door. That one's stuck.'

When he opened the kitchen door, he saw a tall woman with a face like an angry horse staring accusingly at him.

'The blue lamp is over the front door,' she snapped, 'so as a servant of the public, you should have unstuck it.'

This, thought Hamish, must be Mrs Wellington's reforming niece. 'I am not interested in marriage,' he said.

'Are you mad? I am Ruby Souter.'

'I am sorry. The minister's wife has been threatening to send along a good woman to reform me. You're the advocate.'

'That's me. Let's talk.'

Well, thought Hamish after Ruby had left, I wanted to talk it over with someone and never have I had such a grilling in my life. I'm surprised Angela even remembered to call her. Hamish phoned Charlie and said he was going to go over to Drim and that he would ring him if there was anything urgent.

But before he went, Hamish called a second cousin who worked as a stockbroker in Glasgow and asked him to find out if a man called Ebrington Hanover had sold off Lady Jane sanitary towels. He waited for a reply and was relieved to find out that Handy had told him the truth.

The weather was still fine and Drim looked less menacing than usual, although most of the waters on the long finger of loch were black because the towering mountains kept out the sun. He threw sticks for the dogs at the edge of the loch and then strolled up to the castle to be greeted by Handy.

'I thought you'd forgotten me,' said Handy. 'Come in.'

Hamish looked up at the scaffolding. 'Who was working on the buildings and when were they last here?'

'A firm from Invergordon. They stopped for the winter. It's just a job of repointing, mostly.'

'What's the name of the firm?'

'Comstock Builders. What is this? I know. You're worried about the murders. So am I.'

Hamish followed Handy into his study. 'Freda's left me to go back to Glasgow. I'm thinking of getting a housekeeper. Any suggestions?'

'You have a cleaner, haven't you?'

'I get a squad over once a week from an agency in Braikie.'

'Why not some women from Drim? Help the local economy.'

'When a man is single, women around the place are a pest. They all start thinking of marriage. Coffee?'

'Yes, thanks. About the murders. Ruby Souter is going to defend the smugglers.'

'Then you'd better hope they had nothing to do with the murders because Ruby will get them off. There is nothing in the world more terrifying than the sight of a female Scottish ball-breaking advocate in full fight. I know what's worrying you. No weapon. No real proof. I've asked around. No connection to the professor although the idea is that he chanced upon them. Here's your coffee. Help yourself to milk and sugar.'

'There is one thing I've been thinking over,' said Hamish. 'We've still got a lot o' Calvinists around and they wouldn't like the idea of the prof telling them that there isn't a God. To them that means no guilt and go forth and sin. Gets their knickers in a right twist.

'I saw the film of him preaching but I was only look-ing for a familiar face and that was when I saw Olivia in the audience. She's very manipulative. Maybe she lured him to the tower in Drim. But she would need to know the wails and hauntings were fake.'

Both fell silent. At last Hamish said, 'I'd like a look at the Strathbane film again. I saw the bit they showed on television. I wonder about the bits they didn't show. I mean maybe someone threatened him. I think I'll go and have another talk to the producer.'

'Give me a moment and I'll come with you,' said Handy.

He saw Hamish hesitate. 'Bless the man!' cried Handy. 'Hamish, you think I might be your murderer.'

'Something like that,' mumbled Hamish, embarrassed.

'So how better than a close study. Off you go. I'll join you outside.'

What if he is a murderer, thought Hamish uneasily. He could bump me off up on the moors and no one would ever suspect him.

But when Handy climbed into the passenger seat, he seemed his usual affable self.

'The trouble is,' said Handy, 'that policemen, however retired they may be, always have something of the villain about them. Drive on. I'm not going to kill you.' He gave a stage laugh. 'Not today, anyway.'

They were told at Strathbane Television that producer Diarmuid Lancey was in the canteen.

Diarmuid did not look at all pleased to see them, as he was just about to demolish a large steak pie and chips smothered in brown sauce. 'You'll just need to wait,' he said crossly. 'I'm famished.'

Hamish leaned back and looked at the ceiling to avoid the sight of Diarmuid with bits of pie and other detritus sticking to his black beard. He washed the lot down with a large mug of tea, burped loudly, and finally rose to his feet. 'Come on, then,' he said. 'I'm a busy man. Got a special to finish. *Save a Hedgehog for Posterity*. Gripping stuff. Goes out at prime time. Introduced by thon model, Fiona Morris. Opening shot: She's wearing nothing but hedgehogs. That'll get the punters.'

'Beavers might have been a more appropriate subject,' murmured Handy.

'Here, mac, you taking the piss?'

'Not me,' said Handy quickly. 'Just worried folk might think it cruelty to hedgehogs.'

'They're *toy* hedgehogs. Geddit?'

'Got it.'

'You want to see the outtakes, do you?' asked Diarmuid.

'Please,' said Hamish.

'I'll turn you over to Liz here. I've got more important things to do.'

Liz was a flat-chested girl with bright-orange hair and thin, stick-like arms covered in tattoos. 'Here yiz are,' she said in a thick Glaswegian accent.

'Stop there,' said Hamish suddenly. He and Handy looked. A man was on his feet, waving a Bible and shouting something.

'Oh, him,' said Liz. 'The researcher on this was Kyle Kennedy. I'll get him.'

They waited until she returned with a youth with a shaven head, a Fu Manchu moustache, and a bad case of acne.

'Can we get out of here?' demanded Handy suddenly. 'We'll come back in a bit, Liz. Why don't we all go to the pub?'

The young people agreed with delight. 'The room was too small,' Handy muttered to Hamish. 'Gives me claustrophobia.'

In the pub, Handy bought the drinks: a Tequila Sunrise for Liz and a Harvey Wallbanger for Kyle. Hamish said he'd have a tonic water, and Handy bought himself a half of lager.

Questioned about the man with the Bible, Kyle said he was a minister, George Douglas from Howrie.

'Where the hell is Howrie?' asked Handy.

'Wee village outside Strathbane on the Lairg road.'

'So why didn't that bit get shown on TV?' asked Hamish.

'Because he threatened to sue.'

'But he couldn't have sued,' said Hamish.

'Aye, well, but . . .' Kyle looked down at his large baseball boots.

'Oh, I'll tell them,' said Liz. 'Diarmuid is on the road out. He does lousy work. That so-called documentary

126

ended up as a clip on a news item. Don't tell him I told you.'

'There's a gang called Warriors for Christ. Maybe they biffed the prof. Hey, why are you asking? I thought the murders were solved.'

'They are,' said Hamish quickly. 'We're working on another case. Where can I find these Warriors for Christ? What are they like?'

'I never met them. I got a flyer through the door one day. It was about a meeting at someplace or other.'

'Thanks. We'll look into it.'

Hamish and Handy decided to go straight to the village of Howrie. There aren't very many pretty villages in the far north of Scotland, and Howrie was no exception. Apart from the fact that it straggled on either side of the road to Lairg, it was in the cliff-like shadow of tall pillared mountains. Hamish guessed that very little sunlight could manage to shine on the little grey houses. 'It's a sort of mountain burqa,' said Hamish. 'No sunlight. No vitamin D. I wonder if the children have rickets.'

'I think that's the kirk over there,' said Handy. Hamish drove up to a plain, low, whitewashed building with a board outside proclaiming it to be THE CHURCH OF THE RISEN REDEEMED. 'Do you belong to the kirk?' asked Handy.

'I'm not anything really,' said Hamish. 'Let's hae a look.'

They walked around the building. The air was cold. Hamish examined a notice board. 'Here we are. "Warriors for Christ will meet at the community centre in Braikie on Friday 30th at 7 p.m." That's today. We'll go over and join them later. Does this minister have a manse? Can't see anything that looks like one. I'll chap at one o' the doors and ask.'

He knocked at the nearest door. A woman holding a baby answered it. Two children were huddled at her skirts. Her hair was greasy, her skin bad, and her eyes, weary.

'I'm no' buying anything,' she said.

'I'm looking for the minister.'

'Oh, hellfire Geordie. Up the back lane there. Brown place.'

The 'brown place' turned out to be a square sandstone building. It was Victorian and large, dating from the days when the reverends had large families.

They rang the doorbell and waited. Sounds of children and a baby wailing came from inside. At last the door was opened by a very small woman wearing an old-fashioned pinafore. Her lank hair was scraped on top of her head. Tired eyes stared up at them through very thick glasses.

Hamish introduced himself. 'You'd best come in,' she said, scraping a stray tendril of hair from her face.

They followed her through to a large old-fashioned kitchen. There were eight children there, ranging, Hamish guessed, from age twelve years to a few months.

'Is it Mrs Douglas?'

128

'Yes.

'Are you child minding, Mrs Douglas?'

'No. They are all mine.'

'Why don't you sit down,' said Handy. 'I'll make us all a nice cup of tea.'

Mrs Douglas sat down suddenly. 'I can't remember when anyone last waited on me. That would be kind.'

To Hamish's amazement, Handy made tea and chatted with the children, showing them tricks, deftly lifting the wailing baby from its cot and jiggling it up and down until the crying ceased.

Hamish had been talking about the weather and about Lochdubh, but as soon as Mrs Douglas had a cup of tea in her hand, he asked, 'Did your husband ever actually meet Professor John Gordon?'

She smiled, showing vestiges of the pretty girl she had once been. 'You mean the Antichrist? No. He and some members of his congregation planned to go to Golspie and disrupt the lecture but by that time, the professor was dead.'

'Is your husband prone to violence?' asked Handy suddenly.

'He's like most men,' she said wearily. 'He's all right if you don't cross him.'

'I have a castle over at Drim,' said Handy. 'I am sure the children would like to see it.'

The children stared solemnly at their mother. A little girl clutched her mother's apron and whispered, 'Daddy wouldnae like it.'

129

'Just for an hour,' she said. 'But he usually stays on in Braikie for the meeting this evening.'

Hamish wondered how on earth they were going to get the family over to Drim but Mrs Douglas turned out to have an old Volkswagen bus parked at the back of the manse.

Hamish had no chance to ask Handy what he thought he was playing at because Handy opted to travel in the minibus.

Once at the castle, Hamish watched as the children climbed out. He let his dogs out and that caused a sudden rush of children, desperate to pet the animals.

The eldest boy bent down to pat the poodle and his short T-shirt rode up, displaying angry red weals on his back. Hamish's heart sank. He was sure the boy had been beaten. The children were too silent and cowed.

Hamish drew Handy aside. 'We've got a problem. It looks as if the reverend is a wife-beater.'

'And judging by the number of kids, a wife-rapist as well,' said Handy. 'Find out from wifie if her man was ever heard threatening the life of the prof. I'll look after this lot and you get over to Braikie and put the fear o' God into the bastard. I'll try to get her to talk and if she tells the truth, I'll phone you and you can arrest him.'

On the road to Braikie, Hamish reflected that Handy would not get anywhere with Mrs Douglas. Eight children probably meant the abuse had gone on a long time. Or maybe it was just the lad who had been beaten.

It was too early for the meeting when he got to Braikie. He could have visited Dick and Anka but their happiness depressed him so he parked up on the moors in the soft gloaming, closed his eyes, and fell asleep.

He was woken an hour later by the shrill ring of his mobile phone. It was Handy. 'Got her to cough up,' he crowed. 'I got photos of her bruises, one kid has a burnt hand where the bastard held it over the stove, others have marks of beating, and – get this – the six-year-old says Daddy often gets into bed with them for what he calls a wee cuddle. Got it all on tape.'

'Why now?' demanded Hamish.

'Frightened to death. No money. Cut off from friends and family for years. She can stay here. You arrest him and we'll take it from there.'

Hamish phoned Charlie and gave him directions. 'I have a funny feeling I am going to need some muscle,' he said.

'We should have asked the wife for a photo,' said Hamish as they waited outside the hall.

'You seem to be expecting a fight,' said Charlie. 'Why? I mean, this is a lot of wee churchie menfolk.'

'In my bitter experience, it's the wife-beaters who think they're Samson,' said Hamish. 'Here they come, all in black like a bunch o' hoodie crows.'

Six men were approaching the hall. They were all wearing black suits. All had glasses and flat caps. 'The Stepford men arrive,' murmured Hamish as he stepped

131

forward to meet them. 'Which one of you is Mr George Douglas?'

'I am,' said one of them, stepping forward.

'Mr George Douglas,' said Hamish, 'I am arresting you on a charge of wife-beating and cruelty to children. You do not . . .'

That was as far as he got. The reverend was a small man, but he leapt, hands like claws, aiming for Hamish's eyes. Hamish sidestepped, seized his arm, and twisted it up his back. 'To me, brothers,' shrieked Douglas. 'In the name of Christ, lend me aid!'

Hamish thought afterwards that it had all been like an attack by the Seven Dwarfs. The county of Sutherland boasts some of the tallest men in Britain, but perhaps this coven of wife-beaters might be vicious because of their size.

By the time they had all six of them handcuffed and seated against the wall of the hall and waiting for backup, Hamish had a scratched face and Charlie's uniform was torn.

'So much for the Warriors for Christ,' said Hamish. 'What a stramash! I nearly used my Taser. The only thing that stopped me was fear one of those sods would have a heart attack. And it's going to be a long night.'

'Why?' asked Charlie. 'When the lot arrive from Strathbane with the wagon, we get rid o' this lot, type up our reports, and go to bed.'

'We can't say we were still investigating the murders,' said Hamish. 'Say we had an anonymous tip-off of wife-beating and child cruelty in Howrie. So we need the names and addresses of the other men to check up on their families.'

'We could leave that bit until tomorrow,' said Charlie hopefully.

'I'd like to get over to Howrie first in case some of this unlovely lot make bail.'

'All right,' said Charlie reluctantly, and then felt guiltily that his friendship with the colonel was making him soft. He missed his usual dinner and chat at the castle. He enjoyed his odd days fishing with the colonel.

But assaulting police officers was considered serious enough for the six men to be put in the cells to await their appearance at the sheriff's court in the morning. Also, the news of Daviot's odd praise of Constable Charlie Carter had filtered down to Blair, who was only just back in favour with his boss and wanted to keep it that way.

Hamish and Charlie considered it safe to return to Lochdubh and tackle the battered-wife cases in the morning, neither of them thinking for a moment that another murder would drive the wife-beatings out of their minds and bring terror back to Sutherland.

Chapter Seven

When constabulary duty's to be done
The policeman's lot is not a happy one.
—Sir William Gilbert

Hamish realized the next morning, when Jimmy Anderson phoned him, that he had not once stopped to consider that if the smugglers had not committed the murders, it would mean there was a murderer still out there.

But as he drove up to the castle to pick up Charlie he found it hard to believe the victim was Selwyn Sinclair.

'Was he strangled?' asked Charlie.

'Jimmy says it looks like a blow to the head.'

'When was he found?'

'This morning. His secretary, a girl called Martha Dundas, was worried because he had failed to turn up the day before for two important meetings and he wasn't answering his home phone or his mobile. So she went to his home. The door wasn't locked. She found him in the kitchen. He had – or somebody had – laid out a tray with two cups and saucers, milk, and sugar.'

'Ruby will be on to the press, I suppose,' said Charlie. 'I mean, this is going to make our boss look foolish. He rushed in to arrest them for the murders without any real evidence.'

'Aye,' said Hamish gloomily. 'He'll have already taken it out on Blair and Blair will be waiting to take it out on us.'

'He lives in a deserted place,' said Charlie. 'Although, mind you, it's just a bittie along the road from Howrie.'

'I wonder how Handy is getting on with all those children?' said Hamish.

'Maybe he fancies wee Mrs Douglas.'

'Shouldn't think so. But the man's got money and it's easier to be a Good Samaritan when you've got money. He can get someone to ferry the kids of school age to Braikie. He can hire a full-time housekeeper. He can pay a lawyer to handle the legal side and get her a divorce.'

'I thought Clarry, the chef who was your constable, fell for a battered woman and married her.'

'Clarry's a soft-hearted romantic. You don't get to be a chief super by being nice and kind. I wonder if he was ever married?'

'I asked around,' said Charlie. 'He was married three times. Amicable divorces.'

'Not many men in the police force stay married to the same woman unless she's a manipulative bully,' said Hamish.

'Aw! Come on! Cannae be the case. Take Daviot.'

'Take him yourself. Wife's a bully. They haven't any children.'

'There's Blair.'

'He's just lucky. She's a strong woman.'

Hamish had no intention of telling Charlie that Mary Blair was an ex-prostitute whom he had coerced Blair into marrying and that Mary was eternally grateful to be off the streets and had also had a useful previous career of handling drunk men.

Hamish turned into the long road leading to Sinclair's home. 'Press and television there already,' muttered Hamish. 'I wonder who leaks stuff to the press.'

'A good few,' said Charlie. 'Get a bit o' money on the side.'

Blair was talking to the press. As Hamish and Charlie joined the listening group, Blair was saying, 'That's all we've got for you now. There will be a further statement at five o'clock this evening.'

An ambulance was at the side of the road where a small, dark-haired girl was being comforted by a female policewoman. 'Thon lassie must be the secretary, Martha Dundas,' said Hamish. 'She looks to be in a right state and I'll bet my boots it's not all shock. There's a lot o' grief and loss there. We'll try to get her address. Hello, Jimmy. Come to give us our marching orders?'

'You got it. Daviot nearly had a heart attack when he got the news. He's lashing out all round. I gather from some of the questions the press were throwing at him afore you came that Ruby's already been in there, mixing things up. We're expecting a visit from the Faceless

Yins o' Police Scotland or whatever that lot who come down like a ton of bricks on you screaming police sloppiness are called. So count yourselves lucky that I've been told to send you back to your sheep and peasantry.'

'Actually, we've got another job around here,' said Hamish. He told him about the battered wives.

'Don't sweat it,' sneered Jimmy. 'Got one o' those last year. Got her to charge the husband, she got a divorce, and she's just married another wife-beater. They're all sick!'

'What a soft-hearted fellow, you just aren't,' said Hamish. 'How long dead was Selwyn?'

'Just a guess. About twenty-four hours. Maybe more.'

Hamish and Charlie spent a frustrating day interviewing women who all, with a mixture of fear and defiance, insisted they were happily married.

'Let's just pack it in,' said Hamish. 'One day, women will wake up to the fact that they don't really need us. A career and a baby out of a lab are the better choices.'

'What about romance?' asked Charlie.

Hamish had a sudden vision of Priscilla Halburton-Smythe and wondered if that feeling of yearning would ever go away.

'Maybe you'll be lucky, Charlie,' he said. 'I'll try to get that secretary's address and we'll pay a call on her tomorrow.'

* * *

It was a calm evening as Hamish drove slowly along the waterfront. The sky was lemon-coloured, a bad sign, heralding gales to come, but for the moment all was still and calm.

Then he noticed his two dogs sitting outside the police station. He parked the Land Rover and got out. Hamish crouched down and patted them. The poodle was trembling and Lugs looked at Hamish almost accusingly out of his odd blue eyes.

Hamish stood up slowly. He unhitched his telescopic truncheon from his belt, and, telling the dogs to stay, he cautiously pushed open the kitchen door.

A woman was standing by the stove, stirring something in a pot. She had dark hair worn down on her shoulders, and her face showed a few wrinkles. Her jaw was pronounced and her mouth, thin. Her low-cut blouse showed an expanse of freckled bosom.

'State your business,' snapped Hamish, 'and explain what the hell you are playing at.'

'I am Heather Lomond,' she said, 'and I am here to look after you.'

'Chust stop what you are doing and get out,' said Hamish, 'and take whatever you are cooking with you or I shall charge you with trespass.'

Heather pulled out a large handkerchief and proceeded to sob into it. Hamish was sure that her eyes were dry. He went into his living room where he had an old armchair on casters. He wheeled it into the kitchen and thrust her down into it before pushing her outside and across the road to the waterfront. 'Don't ever

138

trespass in my station again or I'll arrest ye!' he shouted, to the amusement of Archie Maclean. He went back in only to come out again with a pot full of stew and a box containing wine, rolls, and a covered bowl of sherry trifle. He set the lot down beside her and looked along the waterfront to where Mrs Wellington was standing flanked by the Currie sisters.

Then he went back into the police station and locked the door behind him. In the kitchen, he climbed out of the window and made his way by a circuitous route to the Italian restaurant, followed by the dogs who had got through the door flap.

'What are you doing here?' cried the waiter, Willie Lamont. 'There's a good woman waiting for you at the station.'

'Is the whole village in on the plot?'

'Aye, that's Mrs Wellington's niece you have just cast off like a worn-out sock.'

'The correct expression is a worn-out glove, Willie. Just get the menu and put a sock in it.'

No one ever thinks about men being bullied, thought Hamish, but calmed by a good dinner and half a bottle of wine, he called Mrs Wellington on his mobile and terrified that lady with talk of her niece being within a hairbreadth of trespass charges.

Hamish was aware that he was vulnerable to thoughts of marriage. He had been on the point of proposing to Christine Dalray and had taken her out for a romantic dinner. But it was when she had said that he must start a healthy diet and that she would supervize it that he felt romance beginning to fade. Why was it that every woman who had ever entered his life wanted him to change and become someone different? The trouble was, he thought bitterly, that women didn't seem to understand an unambitious man. *Then find yourself an unambitious woman*, said the voice of his conscience. 'They don't exist,' said Hamish aloud.

'Who don't?' demanded Willie. 'The wee folk?'

'Mind your own business,' said Hamish. 'Get the bill.'

'You'll suffer for it this evening,' said Willie. 'It don't do, disrespecting the wee folk.'

Hamish paid for his meal and walked out into the gloaming, followed by his dogs who had been eating in the kitchen.

The loch had turned to black glass reflecting the first stars. He had a slight feeling of trepidation as he unlocked the door of the police station, but there was no one inside.

Still, as he stood in the kitchen, he experienced a sort of superstitious feeling of dread. The room suddenly seemed to be filled with all the murderers he had known.

He shook himself like an angry animal. He switched on the kitchen light and felt everything return to normal. He made himself a mug of coffee and settled on the sofa in the living room with the dogs beside him. Hamish had a pang of conscience. He should not have been so harsh with Heather. She had been put up to it by her aunt.

The kitchen door opened and a familiar voice cried, 'Anyone at home?'

With a rush of gladness, Hamish recognized the voice of Elspeth Grant. He went out to meet her.

He always felt a little disappointed when he met the 'new' Elspeth instead of the Elspeth who used to be a reporter on the *Highland Times* and wore thrift shop clothes. Now she was a famous TV presenter, with straightened hair and an expensive wardrobe.

'Are you up to cover the murders?' asked Hamish.

'Yes, I've been to Daviot's useless press conference. So it looks as if they've wasted time arresting the smugglers.'

'Take a seat. Want a dram?'

'A wee one. I'm driving.'

'Every time I fetch a bottle out of the cupboard, I expect Jimmy Anderson to appear. Here you are. I'll hae one myself. Slainte!'

'Daviot is not admitting for a moment that they've made a mistake over charging the smugglers with murder.'

'I suppose I can understand that,' said Hamish. 'I can guess that the professor came across them when he was poking around that tower. But he didn't have a car. No car was found nearby. When he was preaching in Strathbane, he was driving a dark-blue Volvo.'

'Have they searched the loch?' asked Elspeth.

'No.'

'That's where I would dump a car. Or up on the moors in a peat bog.'

'But why Drim?' complained Hamish. 'Sutherland is full of much more interesting castles and ruins.'

'I called over there. This retired chief of police, Ebrington Hanover, is an oddball. I couldn't get near him. I know he isn't married and yet the place, from what I could hear, seemed to be full of children.'

'Who answered the door?'

'Great big fellow, built like an Easter Island statue. Could be a retired cop. Had black socks and shiny black shoes. Always a giveaway. Oh, all right. I'll have another small one. It's been a beast of a day. The big boss's latest squeeze is a blonde researcher called Tiffany McSporran. She's built like Dolly Parton. I'm terrified he'll give her my job. He's besotted.'

'You're always frightened someone will get your job but it never happens,' said Hamish soothingly. 'Look, all off the record as usual but I do need to talk this over. Forget about the smugglers. First there's the murder of the professor. That could well have been done by someone like George Douglas, a hellfire minister in Howrie, minister of a church he probably invented. He beats his wife and torments his children. Those are the children you heard at Handy's.'

'Handy?'

'The retired castle owner. He asked me to call him Handy.'

'Don't tell me a high-ranking policeman, however retired, has a soul?'

'Could be. I like him,' said Hamish. 'But he could be acting. Anyway, some religious fanatic could have

142

followed the prof to Drim, biffed him, got rid of his car, and driven off, feeling he had done God's work.'

'So where does Olivia Sinclair come into this scenario. Oh, well. Why not? I'm only up the road at the Tommel Castle. Slainte! Yes, as I was saying, what could be the connection?'

'Maybe drugs. She was seen with the professor at Maggie's Heiland Hame in Inverness. The police are sure drugs are being dealt at Maggie's but every time they raid the place, it's as clean as anything – from drugs, that is. Now Selwyn was about to divorce her. I thought he might have killed her. Olivia was highly manipulative and, I think, the type of woman who likes having power over people.'

'They're a weird bunch over in Drim,' said Elspeth. 'I mean, living at the end of a one-track road in a glen where the sun hardly ever penetrates is enough to drive anyone bonkers. The one person who would be interested in benefitting from the smugglers is Jock Kennedy. That store can't bring in enough money. I mean, don't tell me the residents don't head off for the nearest supermarket.'

'He was running a sort of pub at the back o' the shop,' said Hamish. 'I stopped that. Och, if he was peddling bootleg cigarettes, I'd give him a warning and confiscate them. But now you've got me thinking. Drugs? I can't see Jock going down that road.'

'Could be. An awful lot of money in it. The lads who were arrested were trying to be big time. Where were they going with their cigarettes if their boat hadn't sunk?

What are the names of the drug barons, if they know any, or is it just cigarettes? They can get more money out of cigarettes than drugs these days.

'Let's get back to your friend Handy. Oh, I will have another whisky. I can always walk. What was I saying? Ah, yes. Look here, Hamish. This man rose to be a chief superintendent in Glasgow where, I assure you, you have to be as tough as old boots to survive in the police force and as cunning as a snake to rise up in the ranks.'

'So what's this menagerie got to do with anything?' asked Hamish.

'Why has he gone all altruistic and filled his castle with snotty bairns and a battered wife? And come to think of it, why Drim? Why would a city man choose Drim of all places? You know there are crooked cops, Hamish.'

'But he called me in to solve the odd wailing sounds. And if he had killed the prof, he wouldn't want me poking around the place.'

'Maybe you're flattered because he's so friendly,' said Elspeth, her odd Gypsy eyes gleaming silver. 'Go over there tomorrow and look at him afresh, as if he's a suspect. How did he get his money anyway?'

'His father was Lady Jane sanitary towels. Handy wouldn't go into the business so the father left it to Handy's brother, who conveniently died. Handy got the lot and sold the business and was able to retire.'

'And what did Handy's brother die of?' asked Elspeth.

'I don't know,' said Hamish, exasperated. 'Why would he kill Selwyn?'

'You said his wife was a manipulator. Maybe she found out something and left a note of it behind and Selwyn found it and challenged Handy.

'Think about it.' Elspeth got to her feet. 'Goodness. I shouldn't have drunk so much.'

Hamish looked at her steadily. 'You could stay here.'

Hazel eyes locked with silver eyes.

And then the kitchen door crashed open and Mrs Wellington bounded in like some animated tweed animal.

'I should have known you would be philandering again after breaking poor Heather's heart.'

'Have you gone mad, woman?' roared Hamish. 'The first time I ever saw the lassie, she had trespassed here, uninvited.'

'She said you kissed her!'

'Havers. Look, do I have to sue the pair of you to get any peace? I wheeled her out in an armchair and left her on the waterfront. Archie Maclean saw me. Ask him. He'll tell you I was so damn furious, I'd rather have kissed a cow's arse.'

'There is no need to be so coarse.'

'Also,' said Hamish, 'you are interrupting my conversation with Miss Grant. You . . .'

He looked wildly around but Elspeth had disappeared. He ran out of the station. There was no sign of a car parked outside. He loudly cursed all women.

'May God forgive you,' said the minister's wife who was just leaving the station.

* * *

145

Hamish tried to phone Elspeth the next morning, only to be told at the hotel that she had left with her crew for Glasgow. But what she had said about Handy worried him.

When Charlie arrived at the station, he told him about his concerns and suggested they go to Drim and call on Handy. 'After that,' said Hamish, 'let's try to have a word with that secretary lassie, Martha Dundas, if we can do it without Strathbane finding out. Och, we're damned up here as being as old-fashioned as Sherlock Holmes. No DNA for us. No high-tech, or someone will report us to Strathbane for muscling in. Nothing but our brains and to tell the truth, Charlie, mine are feeling a bit scrambled at the moment and I've got the first hang-over I've had in ages. Let's go!'

At the castle, Mrs Douglas answered the door. She had her hair brushed down on her shoulders and was wearing pink lipstick. Bad signs, thought Hamish. She's already viewing Handy as her knight on a white charger. 'Mr Ebrington is in his study,' she said.

'We know the way,' said Hamish. But before he or Charlie could reach the study, they were met by Sheila Haggis and Edie Aubrey asking if they would like coffee.

'We'll let you know,' said Hamish. 'Are the children at school?'

'No,' said Edie. 'It's the half term.'

'Then where are they?'

'In the lounge watching telly. They weren't allowed telly at home.'

146

'It is a grand day,' said Charlie. 'They should be outside in the fresh air.'

'What do you precious pair know about bringing up children?' demanded Sheila, her hands on her hips.

'About as much as you,' said Hamish, 'except we aren't lazy. If you'll get out of our way, we're here to see Handy.'

Hamish knocked at the study door and, without waiting for a reply, walked in followed by Charlie.

'Oh, thank God it's only you,' said Handy. 'What on earth have I done?'

'Can't you send them home? Surely Mrs Douglas has taken out an injunction against her husband.'

'The lawyer saw to that and he's handling her divorce. But she doesn't want to go back to the village because she's frightened his pals will have a go at her. Why did I do it? Trying to book a place in heaven? You know something? I don't even like children. Why should I? Nasty little savages with their unformed brains.'

'There is a solution,' said Hamish. 'Rent Mrs Douglas a house in Braikie near the school. Do it today and be shot of the lot of them.'

'You're a genius, Hamish. I'll get hold of the Douglas woman and take her into Braikie right now.'

'Hang on a minute, Handy. Just a few questions. Why do you think Selwyn was killed?'

'Olivia might have found out something or the murderer was frightened that he knew something.'

'You'll forgive me, Handy, but as a policeman, I have

to ask you where you were while he was being murdered?'

'You know where I was. Rescuing this lot.'

'I've been wondering,' said Hamish. '. . . Oh, forget it.'

'He's been wondering,' said Charlie, 'why a tough ex-cop like yourself chose to bury himself in one of the remotest villages of the Highlands?'

'I told you already. I liked the idea of doing up this place and selling it at a profit.'

'But surely you would know nobody would want to buy a castle at the end of the gloomiest loch in the north?' said Hamish.

'Sit down the pair of you,' said Handy. 'But what I tell you is just between us. Promise?'

'If it's got nothing to do with the murders, then you have our word,' said Hamish.

'It was wife number three. Belinda. At first, she seemed the sexiest woman you've ever seen. Then she starts beating me up.'

'You!' Hamish looked amazed.

'Aye. I'd never struck a woman in my life and I was too ashamed to tell anyone. But one night after she had hit me on the head with a bottle, I cracked and I slapped her as hard as I could. She struck the wall and fell unconscious. I phoned for an ambulance. It turned out to be a mild concussion. But maybe I should have hit her before because she demanded a divorce and said she wouldn't contest it.

'But I'd been overworking and overdrinking and I had a nervous breakdown. It was hushed up and I put in for

148

retirement. And just as I'd done that, my brother died and I inherited everything. I had this dream of peace and quiet and seclusion. It hasn't worked out. There's no escaping people.'

'Well, there is,' said Hamish, 'just as long as you don't fill your home with children and a battered wife and two harpies from the village.'

'I'll go now and find somewhere for them in Braikie,' said Handy.

'By the way,' said Hamish, 'what did your brother die of?'

'Heart attack. And I can see poisoning with something rare shining out of your eyes, Hamish. Forget it. Natural death. Let's go.'

While Handy went off with Mrs Douglas to Braikie, the baby and the two smallest children going with her, Hamish and Charlie organized a game of rounders with the other children, sulkily watched by Edie and Sheila.

At last, Hamish and Charlie set off in the direction of Tain, stopping on the way at a roadside catering van to eat bacon sandwiches. Hamish had left the dogs behind. He felt slightly guilty, realizing that when he'd still had the wild cat, he had mostly taken his pets everywhere. He knew it was ridiculous, but he felt that Lugs almost preferred the company of the little poodle to that of the wild cat Sonsie and resented the animal for it.

Hamish thought that it was a long time since he had visited the ancient town of Tain in Ross & Cromarty. Tain is the oldest royal burgh, having been granted a charter in 1066 by King Malcolm the Third of Scotland. Tain was confirmed as a sanctuary, and the centre of the sanctuary was Duthac Chapel. Duthac was an early Christian figure, made a saint in 1499. As they drove along the main street, Charlie remarked that the sanctuary hadn't done Robert the Bruce's wife and daughter any good because Balliol's men had raided the place and taken them prisoner.

'I wish we weren't so conspicuous in this police vehicle,' complained Hamish. 'If a local copper sees us, he'll probably start phoning around to find out what we're doing on his patch. I tell you what, I'll drive out of the town again and park up somewhere and I'll look up Dundas on my iPad.'

'She wouldnae go back to work today, would she?' asked Charlie. 'I mean, we could go to the factory and just ask. They'll hardly start shrieking down the line to Strathbane if we're nice and quiet about it.'

'Good idea,' said Hamish, 'and there's the sign to the industrial estate.'

Sinclair Electronics was in a one-storey modern building, the offices at the front and the factory workshops at the back.

'I wonder who inherits?' said Charlie as they parked at the front and got out.

They walked together into the front office where a languid blonde was reading *Vogue* behind a black leather desk.

On seeing them, she put down the magazine and slowly uncoiled herself from a black leather chair.

'Whit waud yiz be wantin'?' she asked in a harsh voice.

Hired for decoration, thought Hamish. Aloud, he said, 'We would like a word with Martha Dundas.'

'Jist been sent hame. Sick as a bleedin' parrot.'

'And where is home?' asked Hamish. 'Save me phoning headquarters.'

'Lives with her mother. Eighty, Munro Crescent.'

'Thank you.'

'Dinnae mention it, buster. Ta, ta.'

'Well, that was painless,' said Hamish as they both got into the Land Rover. 'Sick, is she? That's an odd way of showing grief. I wonder if she's pregnant. I'll just look up Munro Crescent. Let me see. Tain is Clan Munro territory. Got it. Off we go.'

The crescent turned out to be on the edge of the small town. It comprised a line of red sandstone villas with little gardens in the front of each one. The bushes were all the same, being laurels and rhododendrons on either side of a gravel path. But Martha's front garden boasted, of all things, a palm tree: a miserable, stunted thing that seemed to crouch by the gate, dreaming of sunnier climes. A chill wind shook its dry fronds.

'Poor thing,' said Charlie, patting its trunk. 'Do you think trees get reincarnated, Hamish?'

151

'I don't even know if humans come back, Charlie. Cheer up. Maybe this tree will come back in a new life in Saudi Arabia, standing tall in the sunshine.'

The front door was of polished wood with stained-glass panels. There was a brass knocker in the shape of a pixie. Charlie seized it and performed a heavy rat-a-tat and one brass leg of the pixie fell off. As the door opened to reveal a red-eyed Martha Dundas, Charlie stuffed the metal leg in his pocket.

'Miss Dundas,' began Hamish. 'Is it possible to have a wee word with you?'

She bowed her head by way of assent. They followed her into a front room where a middle-aged woman with aubergine hair was knitting at something long and grey.

'It's the police, Ma,' said Martha. 'Want a wee word.'

Her mother rose to her feet. 'I'll put the kettle on.' She was wearing patent-leather stilettos. Widow, thought Hamish, back out on the hunt for a man.

'Sit down,' said Martha. The room was cold. It was furnished with a beige three-piece suite, a glass-topped coffee table, a large television screen, and a Victorian fireplace on whose hearth sulked a dismal fire. The wind suddenly screeched outside and the palm tree sent its leaves to rap at the glass as if trying to get into the warmth of the room.

'Why a palm tree?' asked Charlie.

Martha raised her eyebrows. 'Did you call to ask me about the garden?'

'Not the climate for it,' pursued Charlie, ignoring glares from Hamish.

'My late father was a great horrorcultured man.'

'I should have guessed that,' said Hamish, used as he was to Willie Lamont's malapropisms and translating *horrorcultured* into *horticulturist* in his mind. 'Now, often in these cases, it helps to know the character of the murdered man. How would you describe Mr Sinclair?'

She took out a lace-edged handkerchief and dabbed her eyes. Hamish was fascinated, wondering where on earth someone these days could even buy a lace-edged handkerchief.

'Mr Sinclair was a saint,' she said.

'Could you try to draw a better picture?' pleaded Hamish.

'He was always kind and considerate. That dreadful wife of his sometimes dropped in, just to make trouble, but as Selwyn said to me after one of her visits, "It would not look good, Martha, if the boss were to lose his temper in front of the staff."'

'Can you think of anyone who might have wanted to kill him?' asked Hamish.

'It's those smugglers!'

'It cannae be them,' said Charlie. 'They're a' locked up.'

'But I saw that Ruby lawyer woman on the telly, and she was saying as how they were silly amateurs and that the real smugglers were murderers.'

'Say that's the case,' said Hamish patiently, 'why on earth would they kill the owner of an electronics factory?'

'I saw this interesting programme on the telly,' said Martha eagerly, 'and it said how this man was suspected of making timers for bombs in his factory so the secret agents bumped him off.'

The door opened and Mrs Dundas tottered in carrying a heavy tray. Charlie stood up to help her.

'Sit down, Charlie,' barked Hamish and rushed to help with the tray himself, terrified that clumsy Charlie might break something. And the contents of the tray did look breakable. The cups were embellished with roses and had gold edging. An Eiffel Tower of a cake stand wobbled precariously. Hamish seized it and put it down on the coffee table.

It was to be a traditional afternoon tea. The bottom of the cake stand held thin slices of bread and butter. The next tier had currant scones, and the top held cream cakes topped with pink icing.

To Hamish's relief, Charlie refused both tea and cakes. The teacups were so fragile that he was frightened of breaking them himself.

Hamish turned his attention to Mrs Dundas. 'Did you meet Mr Sinclair?'

'Aye, a few times. If it was wet or snowy, he'd give Martha a lift home.'

'Don't you have a car, Miss Dundas?'

'Harriet Munro lives at the end of the crescent and she usually gives me a lift.'

'So, in bad weather, why was it necessary for your boss to run you home?'

'We often worked late,' said Martha.

'Did you ever socialize with him? Dinner dates, that sort of thing?'

'Even if he had wanted to, he couldn't,' she said. 'He wanted a divorce and he said he had enough proof of her infidelity and she wasn't going to get any proof of his.'

She turned brick red. 'I mean, we weren't having an affair, but working late and all might look like that.'

Hamish covertly studied her from under his long lashes. She had a neat little figure and thick brown hair worn with a fringe in front and combed down on her shoulders. Her eyes were large and brown. But she was as thick as two planks, thought Hamish, and if Sinclair wasn't using her for sex, what other use to the boss of a thriving business could she be?

'Did you handle all his correspondence?' asked Hamish.

'Harriet, the one at the end of the crescent, her what I told you about, she helped out. A sort of sub-secretary.'

'You boys are not eating any cakes,' exclaimed Mrs Dundas.

'I'm sorry. I don't usually have my tea until later,' said Charlie.

'I'll pack some up for you. Come into the kitchen, laddie, and give me a hand.'

When the door had closed on them, Martha said viciously, 'She'll try to kiss him. I was going to move out and then this happened. How the hell can I hope to get married when I've got a mother who makes a pass at everything in trousers?'

'Could you have afforded a flat on your salary?' asked

155

Hamish, wondering if the late Selwyn Sinclair was planning a little love nest.

'Ma said she would give me a down payment on a mortgage.'

Hamish stood up. 'Miss Dundas. If you can think of anything at all that might be useful, do call me.' He handed her his card.

In the little hall, he shouted for Charlie, who emerged from the back premises holding a cake box. 'You've got lipstick on your face,' whispered Hamish. Aloud, he thanked Martha for her time and then asked, 'What's the number of Harriet's house?'

'Twenty-five. It's the last on the left.'

In the Land Rover, Charlie tenderly laid the cake box on the backseat and scrubbed the lipstick from his face.

'Awfy embarrassing woman, that mother,' he said.

'Desperate to find another husband, I think,' said Hamish. 'Let's hope Harriet Munro is a bit more intelligent.'

Chapter Eight

Sigh no more, ladies, sigh no more,
Men were deceivers ever
                                          —Shakespeare

Harriet Munro was a small troglodyte of a woman. She was barely five feet high. Thick black hair grew low on her forehead. Her bushy eyebrows met in the middle and she had peroxided an incipient moustache, which had resulted in a bright-orange line above her upper lip. Her figure appeared dumpy but that could have been because of her baggy clothes. But her eyes were large and brown with flashes of green.

'We are investigating the murder of Mr Sinclair,' said Hamish after the introductions had been made.

'Oh, aye. Come ben. Tea?'

'No, thank you, we're all right.'

'In here.' She pushed open a door. An elderly man with silver hair and gold-rimmed glasses put down a copy of the *Guardian* newspaper and said in a high fluting voice, 'Why are the police here?'

'Because o' the boss's murder.'

'I'll leave you to it.' He hurried from the room.

'My father's the auld geezer,' said Harriet. 'Used tae be a civil servant. Retired now. Take a seat.'

Hamish sat down in a comfortable wing armchair and looked around. It was a pleasant room with a bright fire on the hearth and the walls lined with books.

'We are interested in the character of Mr Sinclair.'

'Oh, him? Poor Martha.'

'Why poor Martha?'

'All he wanted was a bit on the side. He paid me a good wage to cover up for her mistakes. Martha was sure he meant to marry her when he got a divorce, but I'd seen the wife. I mean, Martha's hardly a glamour puss.'

'There are lots of pretty girls in the Highlands,' said Charlie.

'But not all of them are happy to be screwed on the office carpet. I asked her if he ever even took her out for dinner and she said he couldn't until the divorce came through. She wouldnae listen, the poor wee tart. He was a good businessman. I mean, the place is a success.'

'You wouldn't happen to know who inherits?'

'His cousin, Malcolm Warrington. He's got his own electronics place down in Renfrew so everything will go on as usual except for Martha. I can't see any normal boss putting up with her.'

'She must have something special,' protested Charlie.

Harriet shrugged. 'Young and ready.'

'Would he have gone in for any shady dealings?'

'No, all above board. I know as much about that company as if I was on the board, believe me.'

Hamish felt a sudden pang of pity for her. He wanted to tell her to slim, shave her eyebrows, go to a good beautician. It was a hard world when a lassie with a fine brain could be left on the shelf.

He said as much to Charlie after they had left. 'There are quite a lot o' lassies don't want to come off the shelf these days,' he said.

'You mean, careers last, men don't?'

'Aye. Lots of drunkenness and wife-beating around.'

'I still can't figure out Handy,' said Hamish. 'He bothers me.'

'Let's get a bite to eat,' suggested Charlie.

They stopped at a café and had pie and peas and chips washed down with Irn-Bru, a soda often called Scotland's other national drink. 'That was right grand,' said Charlie when they had finished. 'I get so many gourmet meals up at the castle, I sometimes long for some real cheap cholesterol-building food.'

'Let's call on Handy tomorrow,' said Hamish. 'I've missed something. It's getting late. You won't be able to eat any gourmet dinner tonight.'

'Not invited. George and the missus are suffering the Daviots this evening.'

'I'd never have thought that snobbish wee colonel would go to such lengths as to protect you.'

'Hamish, I won't hear a word of criticism about George. Not one! Anyway, maybe you'd like to come back with me.'

'Priscilla?'

'Aye, she's up for a few days.'

'Got some pillock of a boyfriend with her?'

'No. On her own.'

When they arrived at the Tommel Castle Hotel and were settled in Charlie's flat, Hamish suddenly realized that Priscilla was probably having dinner with the chief superintendent and his wife. He said, 'I cannae get that lassie Harriet Munro out of my mind.'

Charlie stretched his large boots to the blaze of the peat fire. 'You mean there was something about her other than her looks?'

'I think myself pretty bright,' said Hamish, 'but thon lassie, well, I sense a huge brain at work there. I bet she could run that factory herself.'

'It's Scotland, she's a woman, she's no Cleopatra, so she hasn't a hope in hell of being anything other than a dogsbody. Do you think she could have killed Selwyn?'

Hamish laughed. 'Not for a moment. But I'm going back to see her soon. I want to talk over the case with her.'

'You've got me,' said Charlie huffily. 'And Priscilla.'

'I know. But I would like to pick that brain of hers. Look. I'm kept out of the loop. No forensics. No DNA. No mysterious dust from the Amazon basin. All I've got really is my copper's instinct. Dammit. It's a hunch. I'll take Harriet out for dinner. I've got a second cousin who's just joined the force in Glasgow. I'll see if I can get him.'

Hamish phoned. Charlie heard him say, 'It's me,

Hamish Macbeth, Dougal. Could you do something for me? Can you find any savvy businessman down there who could discover if Lady Jane sanitary towels ... *no, it is not a joke*. Stop sniggering. Find out if the company was actually sold for a lot of money. What do you get out o' it? Tell you what, be a good laddie and I'll get you an intro to Elspeth Grant. Aye, promise.

'Now, let's wait and see,' Hamish said to Charlie.

When Priscilla called at the police station the following morning, it was to find Hamish had left. She was puzzled, because the hotel staff had told her that Hamish had been in Charlie's flat the evening before.

She turned away to get into the car and gave a start of surprise to find Mrs Wellington, the Currie twins, and a woman she did not know, all glaring at her.

'We are here to show you an example of the perfidy of Hamish Macbeth,' intoned Mrs Wellington.

'Mrs Wellington,' said Priscilla firmly, 'you have been wrong about Hamish many times before and I am sure you are wrong again.'

Heather was thrust forward. 'My niece, Heather, cooked a meal for him out of the goodness of her heart and he threw her out on to the waterfront.'

'How long had Hamish known your niece?'

'He hadn't met her before but ...'

'Are you trying to tell me he went into the police station one day to find a strange woman in command of the kitchen?'

161

'But it wasn't a strange woman, it was my niece,' boomed Mrs Wellington.

'It was right cruel,' said Nessie Currie.

'Cruel,' echoed her sister.

'You're all mad,' said Priscilla. She walked back to her car, got in, and drove off.

The minister's wife looked uneasily at her niece as if seeing her for the first time. Her husband had said to her only the other day, 'What do you think I would feel if I came home and found a strange woman in my kitchen?'

'Maybe we have been a bit pushy,' she said reluctantly.

'I think it's time I was getting back to my own place,' said Heather sulkily. The sight of the beauty of Priscilla had made her feel grubby and stupid although she would never admit it to herself.

Hamish pulled over to the side of the road to answer his mobile phone. It was Dougal from Glasgow.

'You were asking about Lady Jane,' he said. 'Well, when the factory was sold, any money went to pay off miles of outstanding debts. The father had let the son run it and he pretty well gambled and drank it into the ground.'

'I heard he was the saintly one,' complained Hamish.

'Not from what I've heard.'

When Hamish rang off, he did not start to drive immediately but sat staring out at the long expanses of moorland rising up to the mountains.

'What's up?' asked Charlie.

Hamish told him.

'He cannae be a villain,' said Charlie. 'He was the one who asked us over to investigate.'

'Look at it this way, Charlie. Drim is on my beat and sooner or later I would ha' paid the place a visit and asked about all the crossed rowan branches. So he gets us over. The prof's body was down in that basement. We weren't supposed to find it. I don't think it's cigarettes. I think it's drugs and Maggie's is the tie-up.'

'This is Handy, Hamish. He's not a killer surely? And what's it got to do with Selwyn?'

'Selwyn could have found something going through his wife's papers. He accuses Handy of dealing her drugs and Handy breaks his skull.'

'But surely one of the villagers would have seen a ship or boat of some kind in the loch?'

'Not necessarily. The stuff could be offloaded outside and taken overland to the castle. There was no search made of the castle because of his old rank. I wonder.'

'Wonder what?'

'He does this philanthropic act of rescuing Alice Douglas. He might worry that I would get suspicious one of these days. So he seizes the opportunity of an excuse to find her a house in Braikie and what better place to store the stuff?'

'But didn't you suggest he find a place for her?'

'Aye, but the way he was moaning on, it was an obvious suggestion to make.'

'So what do we do now?' asked Charlie.

'We go to Braikie, that's what. There is Gladwells, the main estate agent.'

'If we find the house and Handy is there, what do we do?'

'Back off until he disappears. We'd best go back and change out of our uniforms and take your old car, Charlie.'

Hamish learned that Handy had rented a large villa near the school. I hope I am wrong, he thought. That poor woman must think she's in heaven and it will all come falling about her ears.

The sky had turned dark to suit his mood. They parked up a farm track behind the villas, concealing the car in a stand of trees. They made their way along the back of the villas until they located the one called The Cedars. They had been told it was the one at the end of the cul-de-sac.

'I can hear men's voices,' said Hamish. 'But I've got to get nearer.'

'Let's take a punt on it,' whispered Charlie.

'What do ye mean?'

'Let's phone in and say drugs are being stored in that villa. Anonymous tip-off. Right?'

'It could work,' whispered Hamish. 'Tell them the men are armed. That'll bring them.'

They retreated to where they had left the car, and Charlie spoke urgently to headquarters. 'You don't often bring the dogs with you,' said Charlie.

'I haven't got over losing Sonsie.'

'That poodle's a wee darling.'

'Talk about something else.'

'I've just remembered. When I went to collect my car at the hotel, Clarry gave me a packet of ham sandwiches and a flask of coffee.'

'Great! Wheel it out.' They ate contentedly, but after half an hour Hamish began to fret. 'Where the hell are they?'

Charlie opened the car window. 'Right up there. Helicopter's just arrived. Let's go.'

'Wait!' shouted Hamish. 'If you were Handy, supervising his men, and heard the first whir of that copter, you'd head for the airport. Let's get going. Phone the airport and tell them to delay any flights until we arrive.'

Handy was sitting in the London plane at Inverness airport, waiting for takeoff. He looked out and, with a sinking heart, saw Hamish Macbeth and Charlie Carter walking towards the plane followed by airport security.

He meekly allowed himself to be arrested and marched from the plane, all the time trying to figure out ways to escape. He had read up on Hamish's previous cases and had begun to feel uneasy. His do-gooder act in finding that villa for Alice and her children had seemed to him a stroke of genius.

To Hamish's surprise, the police helicopter had just landed and Jimmy Anderson was climbing down, followed by Daviot, Blair, and two policemen. 'Got a call from airport security,' said Jimmy severely. 'I'll take it from here. You can follow by road.'

'Any drugs found?' asked Hamish.

'Cocaine, amphetamines, Ecstasy, you name it. Gang's rounded up. Good work.'

'Be careful, Jimmy. He's wily.'

'So am I. See you at headquarters.'

Handy looked down at the highland countryside from the helicopter. Why had he ever decided to come north? Had it not been for Hamish Macbeth, he could have lived out a comfortable old age.

He would be locked up for life. What would his sister think? He had not waited for the sound of the helicopter before trying to escape. A tip-off from police head-quarters meant he had time to pack and try to disappear. Then he wondered: if he were dead, would they try to hush things up? His arrest would mean a lot of his pre-vious cases would have to be examined and they would hate that. The helicopter began to swoop down towards Strathbane. 'Looks like a big reception down there,' said the co-pilot, opening the door.

'Shut the bloody door!' shouted Jimmy. 'It's freezing.'

Handy wasn't handcuffed. He had allowed himself meekly to be arrested. No one could have guessed what he planned to do. He dived straight through the open window. They watched appalled as his body plummeted to earth.

* * *

Tilly Strachan of Strathbane Television always described herself with a rueful smile as a hard-bitten reporter. She was fond of saying, 'I'm as tough as old boots. It's the men who go to pieces at the sight of a bit of blood.'

She was waiting in the car park of police headquarters with the rest of the press when Handy's body crashed down at her feet. Blood oozed in a widening pool right to Tilly's shoes.

'Get a shot of that,' she ordered the cameraman and then fainted dead away, right across the body, to the fury of the waiting police, headed by Superintendent Daviot.

When Hamish and Charlie arrived some time later they were surprised to be told that they had been booked into the Queen's Hotel in Strathbane and would stay there the night before a meeting to be held in the boardroom in the morning.

Hamish returned to Lochdubh to collect Lugs and Sally, his conscience telling him he had left them alone long enough. Charlie had just arrived in Hamish's room when Jimmy Anderson walked in and headed straight for the minibar.

Hamish watched as Jimmy emptied two miniature whiskies into a glass, drank them down, and reached for two more.

'Hold it!' shouted Hamish. 'That goes on my bill. And when did you lot ever pay extras.'

'Now we do,' said Jimmy. 'You could order champagne and caviar and they wouldnae blink an eye. This is going to be the cover-up of all time.'

'I just saw on the news that Handy jumped out of the helicopter. Why wasnae the man handcuffed?'

'Because he was up in the buggering sky!' howled Jimmy. 'Don't you start.'

He rolled on to the bed with a glass of whisky cradled on his chest and stared moodily at his shoes.

Hamish pulled a chair up beside the bed. 'Uncle Hamish is here. Begin at the beginning and go on to the end.'

'We've got him for the murders as well,' said Jimmy.

'All of them?'

'Well, he said he was sorry about Selwyn but he had to go.'

'And what about the prof and Olivia?'

'Didnae have the time. But, och, it stands tae reason. In the name o' the wee man, have a drink, you sanctimonious pillock.'

'I would ha' liked a whisky but you've taken the lot.'

Jimmy scrabbled on the table beside the bed until he had got the phone. He dialled room service and ordered a bottle of the finest malt whisky.

'Look here,' said Hamish. 'If it's all on expenses, let's go and have something to eat.'

'You go,' said Jimmy. 'I'm not supposed to tell you anything until the morrow. And take your hounds with ye.'

* * *

168

In the dining room, Charlie said, 'I'm surprised you didn't shake more out of him. He'll have passed out by the time we get back.'

'Don't need to. Order your food and then I'll tell you why.'

Hamish ordered trout and a T-bone steak, because 'we are expecting company.'

'What company?' asked Charlie, after he had ordered a mixed grill for himself.

'It's for the dogs,' said Hamish. 'And if you've any of that mixed grill left, I'll put it in a bag I've got with me. So, this is what I pretty much know will happen.

'Tomorrow, we will be threatened with anything they can think of if we breathe a word. It's all going to be hushed up. I mean all. The murders, the drugs. The gang will be charged with possession and get light sentences. Heavy sentences if they breathe a word about Handy. The young gangsters to Ruby's delight will get away with everything. All swept under the carpet, because, if not, all Handy's previous cases from way back will need to be opened again.'

'They cannae do that!' shouted Charlie.

'Keep your voice down.'

'So how do they explain Handy falling out of a police helicopter after being arrested at Inverness airport?'

'It isn't America. We don't put everyone in handcuffs. I am sure someone bent over him and gently led him off the plane and into the helicopter. They'll complain he had a seizure and made for the window and fell out. End of a distinguished, blameless life.'

'I don't know if I can live with this, Hamish?'

'Do you want to leave Lochdubh?'

'No.'

'So live with it. I'll find a way around it.'

They finished their meal. Hamish apologized for the non-appearance of his 'friend' and asked for a doggie bag.

Back in his hotel room, Jimmy was passed out on the bed. 'I've got a twin-bedded room,' said Charlie. 'Leave the scunner where he is.'

A red-eyed Jimmy, smelling horribly of old whisky and sweat, led them to the boardroom the next morning. Daviot came in followed by Blair and several other detectives. Four men in sober black sat in the middle of the table. Strategically placed around the table were bottles of mineral water. A side table held a coffee machine, cups and saucers, milk and sugar, and an array of cakes.

'Eiffel Towers and fly cemeteries,' muttered Hamish. 'Helen is really pushing the boat out.'

Eiffel Tower cakes are those pink confections decorated with shredded coconut, and fly cemeteries are currants sandwiched in short pastry.

'Heven't they heard o' croissants in this pert o' the world?' demanded one of the men in dark suits.

Old-fashioned Kelvinside Glasgow accent, thought Hamish.

Like the biblical hart that panteth after cool waters, Jimmy was steadily drinking Perrier.

One of the men who seemed to be the leader, 'Call me Alexander', began to precisely outline the situation. Much as they would like to charge Ebrington Hanover with everything they could think of, the man was dead and all his past cases had to be left untouched or the jails of Glasgow would be emptied of villains.

'What about the murder of Selwyn Sinclair?' asked Hamish.

'And who are you?'

'Sergeant Hamish Macbeth.'

'Hamish Macbeth what?'

'Sorry. Hamish Macbeth, sir.'

'Well, Macbeth, as he confessed to that murder, it follows he did the others. So that's all over with and don't you forget it. All of you will keep your mouths shut from now on. Where was I before I was so rudely interrupted?' His voice droned on and on while Hamish thought hard. Yes, it follows that Olivia had spilled the beans on her computer, Selwyn Sinclair had found something incriminating and challenged Handy. But the others? Usually when I know that the murderer has been caught, I get a feeling of lightness. But I don't, fretted Hamish.

He sat with his head bowed, wishing the whole farce would soon be over, when to his dismay he heard his name. 'Is Sergeant Hamish Macbeth here?'

'Yes, sir,' said Hamish.

171

'I see from the reports that it was you who suspected Hanover. Why?'

Hamish quickly marshalled his thoughts. If he took the credit, then promotion might occur and promotion meant leaving Lochdubh. Jimmy Anderson's job was at risk. He had heard the suits grumbling about 'that disgustingly smelly detective'.

Hamish stood up and cleared his throat. His highland accent much stronger than usual, he said, 'I considered Mr Ebrington to be a friend and because of his previous high rank would never have suspected him had it not been for Detective Jimmy Anderson. Mr Ebrington claimed his fortune came from the sale of his father's business. Jimmy ordered me recently to find out if that business had been sold for a lot of money. It had not. Then Ebrington had suddenly turned charitable and had rented a large villa for some battered housewife and her eight children. It seemed out of character. So Constable Carter and myself decided to go and have a look. We saw a gang of rough-looking men carrying boxes into the villa. So I phoned Detective Anderson who acted quickly – as he always does, sir, in any emergency. I must apologize to Detective Anderson, sir. Carter and myself gave a little party for him last night and kept him up late.'

'Is Anderson here?'

Jimmy rose shakily to his feet.

'Very good work, Detective. In normal circumstances, you would receive a commendation, but you do understand, these are not normal circumstances.'

'Yes, sir,' said Jimmy meekly.

'In fact, you may take the next few days off. Do you not think so, Superintendent Daviot?'

'Oh, yes, certainly,' said Daviot.

'Wait a wee moment,' howled Blair, lumbering to his feet.

'Who are you?'

'Detective Chief Inspector Blair.'

'What is the reason for this rude interruption?'

'It's that great loon, Macbeth. He solves cases and lets someone else take the credit because he doesnae want to be promoted and lose his wee station in Lochdubh.'

'Is this true, Macbeth?'

Hamish, still on his feet, kept a look of amiable stupidity on his face and said, 'My mither always told me to speak the truth. Do you want me to swear on the Bible, sir?'

'No, no. Daviot, control your staff. There is always some exhibition of jealousy among police officers. Now you may sit down, Macbeth.'

'Oh, thank you, thank you, sirs. Thank you,' gabbled Hamish.

'My dear fellow, I merely told you to sit down. It's not a papal blessing.'

Sycophantic laughter all round, with the glowering exception of Blair.

At the end of a long morning and everyone sworn to secrecy, the monumental cover-up was agreed upon.

Jimmy caught hold of Hamish on the way out. 'Thanks a lot. You saved my job.'

'Aye, well, next time you call, it's herb tea for you,' said Hamish.

'I'm off tae the sauna,' said Jimmy.

'With what you'll sweat off,' said Hamish, 'they could sell it as one-hundred-proof alcohol.'

He and Charlie went back to the hotel. Hamish was just getting into the police Land Rover when his phone rang. It was Priscilla. 'Hamish, have you got your dogs? They were wandering along the waterfront in the cold and rain yesterday afternoon looking for you.'

'I picked them up last night. I'll be with you soon. It's been a big case.'

Hamish told Charlie about the call. 'You've got your Sherlock back,' said Charlie. 'You can tell her about the case.'

'Did you ever smoke, Charlie?'

'Oh, aye, twenty a day.'

'Give up clean?'

'No, my mind would say, "Oh, go on, jist the one", and I'd start the craving up again. Oh, I see what you're getting at. I didnae know it was like that. You ended the engagement.'

Although highland himself, Hamish was often taken aback by other highlanders' gift of a sort of telepathy.

Chapter Nine

They wouldn't be sufficiently degraded in their own estimation unless they were insulted by a very considerable bribe.

—W. S. Gilbert

Priscilla was puzzled. Hamish thanked her effusively for looking after his dogs but insisted on rushing off. She followed Charlie down to his flat and heard all about the hushed-up case and it was only after Charlie had finished, swearing her to secrecy, that she said it looked as if Hamish was definitely avoiding her.

'No, no,' protested Charlie, 'it's just that he's puzzled about the other two murders. Also he doesn't like all the fiddling that's going to go on. Those young hooligans will get off scot-free, lawyer Ruby will be bribed with the offer of getting to be a judge or something. And maybe the only good thing about it all is they'll have to bribe Alice Douglas to keep her mouth shut.'

'Surely it will leak somehow,' said Priscilla. 'He was taken off a plane at Inverness airport. The other passengers will have heard him being charged and seen him put in handcuffs.'

'He was only told to accompany them from the plane. The other passengers would simply think he was some important bigwig being taken off to a meeting.'

Priscilla made for the door. 'I might just drop down to the station to see Hamish.'

'I wouldnae do that,' said Charlie quickly. 'He said he needed some sleep.'

'Pity. I'm only here until tomorrow.'

But Hamish was not asleep. He was heading for Tain to see if he could talk to Harriet Munro. He had sensed in her an acute intelligence. He desperately wanted to discuss the case. To believe Handy guilty of the murders did not seem right. It was Saturday so surely she would not be at work.

Harriet was at home and looked very surprised when Hamish awkwardly asked her if she would come out for dinner with him as he wanted to discuss a case.

'I suppose so,' she said. 'I'll tell Dad.'

In the hope that she would be free, Hamish had booked a table in the restaurant at the Royal Hotel.

When they were seated, Harriet looked at him curiously and asked, 'Why me? I mean, did you suspect me of anything?'

'No, not that. I remembered having guessed you were of above-normal intelligence and my brain's a muddle.'

'We'll order first,' said Harriet, 'and then tell me all about it.'

Both ordered scallops to start with. Then Harriet said she would like lamb shank and Hamish opted for the chicken pie. Harriet said she drank red wine with everything and so he asked for a bottle of Merlot.

And then Hamish began to talk. Harriet was a superb listener, their table was far enough away from other diners to ensure some privacy.

He finished his tale over coffee, warning her again that everything had to be secret.

'We'll pretend that Handy never murdered anyone other than Selwyn,' said Harriet. 'Now, Olivia could cause jealousy, but she was also capable of deep jealousy. Mr Sinclair and I had sometimes been away on business trips when Martha was ill, and Olivia raged into the office one day demanding to see his secretary. When she saw me, she burst out laughing and said, "Darling, I'm sure you cannot possibly have been screwing this hearth rug." I could ha' killed the bitch, but I'm not the killing kind. He never said that Martha was really his secretary. You said she liked to manipulate people. I bet she would have thought it funny to get the prof tied up in knots and get him to sneak up to Drim. And that poor minister. Maybe she lost his faith for him. But there is one point in your story you have missed.'

'What's that?'

'Selwyn Sinclair was a philanderer. He was the sort of man who'd romance a woman, get her tied up in knots, and then dump her. Say there was nothing

177

incriminating in Olivia's notes or computer. What, just what, if Handy found out his sister had been one of Selwyn's victims? She took off for Glasgow, you said. Or it could have been Sheila Haggis. She obviously adored Selwyn.'

'You haven't mentioned Martha,' said Hamish.

'She's been fired. I've got her job, but then, I've been doing it for so long so that Selwyn could pretend Martha was efficient and justify taking her on business trips.'

'Could she have murdered anyone? I mean, Olivia was strangled.'

'All it takes for a woman to do something like that is an unsuspecting victim, a belt, and passion.'

'I've told you all I know,' said Hamish. 'Promise me, you'll have a think about it.'

Harriet smiled. 'I'll try.'

'Why do you let yourself go?' asked Hamish.

To his horror, her eyes filled with tears. 'I'm sorry,' he said hurriedly. 'But with that brain of yours, why don't you do something about your appearance? Are you punishing yourself?'

'You are a sexist pig,' said Harriet, getting to her feet.

'No, listen. Sit down, lassie. You're worth a thousand. But it stands out a mile that you don't care how you look. Why?'

She sat down slowly and stared at the tablecloth. 'I live with my father,' she said. 'He's a retired civil servant. *Civil* is a joke. He's always jeered at me and said Mother must have played him false with an ogre.'

'Has he enough means to support himself?'

'Yes, I've got a woman who comes daily to make his lunch.'

'Then get a flat of your own. After that, you can start to alter your appearance and no one is really going to notice much if you do it a bit at a time.'

'Do you enjoy playing Pygmalion, copper?'

Hamish flushed miserably. 'Sorry. Forget I said anything.'

'Look, thanks for the dinner. I think I would like to go home now.'

Hamish parted from her on her doorstep. He felt miserably that he had been boorish and insensitive.

He tossed and turned that night, wondering and wondering if a woman could be the murderer.

He had planned to enjoy a leisurely Sunday, attending to his hens, geese, and sheep and doing the household chores, but just as he was leaving the henhouse with a bowl of eggs, he heard the sound of approaching female voices. He peered round the end of the Land Rover and saw Mrs Wellington and her niece approaching.

Hamish went hurriedly into the kitchen and locked the door. He went into the living room and lay behind the sofa, cuddling the dogs and whispering to them to be quiet until the knocking at the door ceased and he could hear them moving away.

Damn all women, he thought viciously. I'd better go away somewhere for the day. Not Drim. I have to think. Then he had the idea of driving just one more time to

Ardnamurchan to where he had left his wild cat, Sonsie. Sonsie and Lugs had been great friends. Perhaps if the cat saw Lugs, she might emerge.

He phoned Charlie, who offered to come with him but Hamish refused. 'I'll go somewhere myself,' said Charlie. 'I think Mrs Halburton-Smythe is fed up with me.'

'Why?'

'That one dinner invitation was not enough for Daviot's missus. She's always coming over on one pretext or another.'

'I'll fix it,' said Hamish. After he had rung off, Hamish put his head in his hands and thought long and hard. Then he phoned Daviot. 'What is it, Macbeth?' demanded Daviot.

'It is about your wife's visits to Mrs Halburton-Smythe.'

'What the hell has that got to do with you?'

'You know the Countess of Strathkyle?'

'Not personally.'

'Well, she and Mrs Halburton-Smythe are old friends, bosom buddies, and the countess says that Mrs Halburton-Smythe can't find time because of some copper's wife always hanging around.'

'Outrageous!'

'Aye, but them aristos are always that close. You don't want to find yourself out of the loop, sir.'

'I'll talk to her,' said Daviot.

After he had put the receiver down, Daviot suddenly remembered that at the Highland Games at

180

Drumnadrochit, Hamish had finished competing in the hill race and was accepting the winner's cup from the Earl of Strathkyle. He had seen Hamish later in the tea tent talking to the countess and before he could stop her, his wife had rushed over, only to be quite dreadfully snubbed.

'I introduced myself and she says, "You are interrupting an interesting conversation. Go away,"' his wife had complained. 'I must admit Macbeth looked embarrassed and stood up to leave, but her damn ladyship says, "Oh, sit down and ignore her."'

Daviot squared his shoulders and picked up the phone again. His wife must be told to back off, and that was going to take hours of calming and soothing.

As Hamish drove steadily towards Ardnamurchan, that part of Scotland that has become a Scottish wild cat sanctuary, the weather was proving the story that in the Highlands you can experience four climates in one day. When he set out, the sun was shining. Then there was a blizzard. Then the sun again with a double rainbow straddling the horizon. After that, soft rain followed by a sudden gale, sweeping in from the Atlantic.

Hamish had decided to emulate the days when Dick had been his policeman and take a picnic along with a table, chair, and stove. Having reached Ardnamurchan, he chose a spot as near as he could remember to the area where he had left Sonsie. The wind was still howling, whistling through the heather. He realized it was going to be a long day and he should have waited until evening, but perhaps she was somewhere close. He had brought several paperbacks with him so he knew that unless it grew too cold, he could pass the time quite pleasantly.

He set up an old card table in the shelter of the Land Rover and opened up a canvas chair. He thought again about Dick and then Willie and Clarry, all fascinated by the food business. Although maybe Willie Lamont was more fascinated by the latest cleaners on the market than food. Thank goodness, Charlie didn't have the food bug – except for guga, which didn't count as food, thought Hamish, as it was just as tasty as eating a rubber duck.

He fried a pan of sausages and bacon, setting aside some of it to cool for the dogs before breaking a couple of eggs into the pan. He had a packet of ham and two baps to make sandwiches later.

Why could he not believe that Handy had committed those other two murders?

He turned over his talk with Harriet. Could the murders have been done by a woman? He remembered his criticism of her appearance and shifted uneasily. What on earth had come over him? *Get yourself a man or your life will be wasted?* But he had hurt her and that he could not bear.

He looked at his watch. She would still be at work. He phoned and got through to her. 'I didnae mean to be rude,' he said in a rush. 'I meant, wi' your personality and those eyes, lassie, you could knock 'em all for six.'

'Have you been drinking, copper?'

'No.'

'Then you are stark, raving bonkers.'

Harriet sat, staring at the computer. Her new boss, a CEO appointed by Selwyn Sinclair's brother, Andrew, was easy to work for.

She turned what Hamish had said round and round in her head. But any slight alteration of her appearance would cause her father to make one of his jeering remarks. *Then move out*, said the voice of Hamish Macbeth in her head.

Her boss put his head round the door of her office. 'Still here? I'm off. Thanks for finding us that house. Our old place in Tain had got too small.'

Harriet found herself saying, 'Do you still own it?'

'Yes, why?'

'I might like to rent it, if it's not too expensive.'

'No, no. In fact, we hadn't got around to seeing the estate agent.' He pulled a bunch of keys from his pocket and extracted two. 'Go and have a look. It is Five, The Loan.'

'I'll let you know,' said Harriet, taking the keys. What would her father say? But if she were no longer around, he could say anything he wanted.

Hamish woke up, realizing he had drifted off to sleep. The wind was whistling through the heather with a mournful soughing sound.

It was the time of year when it never really got dark. He whistled, as he used to whistle for Sonsie, but the mocking wind seem to send it flying unheeded across the empty landscape.

This is childish, he thought. If Sonsie's gone feral, good luck. He decided to go to Strathbane to see Jimmy. He suddenly had so many questions. How had the smugglers got the contraband drugs to the castle? Unless the whole village was in cahoots, they must have found a quiet way in without sailing up the loch. The entrance to the tunnel was screened from the village. But that was one way. Because Handy was not a suspect, they'd never thought of another way.

That scaffolding! Hire what looks like a gang of builders, bringing in trucks with equipment from the coast, and who's going to think it odd? The 'hauntings' were also to stop anyone looking too close, until it had amused Handy to bring in the local bobby.

He packed everything up including his dogs and set off, so fired up with this new idea that he failed to look in his rearview mirror where he might have seen a wild cat, sitting by the road, watching him go.

He found Jimmy at his desk, morosely sipping mineral water. Apart from Jimmy, the detectives' room was empty.

'Where is everyone?' asked Hamish.

'Gone off to celebrate the Great Party of Keep Your Mouths Shut.'

'It'll leak, sooner or later,' said Hamish. 'Things always do. Someone tipped Handy off. Who was it?'

'Got it off Handy's phone. One of the secretaries. She's on the run and we've got strict orders not to fire her. Freda's identified the body and has agreed to the quietest funeral in history. She's crying and horrified. Says she knew nothing about it.'

'Believe her?'

'Laddie, I've been *ordered* to believe her. You don't have a flask on ye?'

'Why aren't you in the pub?'

'The Faceless Suits said I was to keep out of the pub or it would be a long stay in rehab on my record. What do you want anyway?'

Hamish told him his theory about the builders. 'Oh, shut that stupid highland face of yours,' said Jimmy. 'No one wants to know anything anymore. They're so paranoid, they may have bugged my desk.'

As he stood up, about to leave, Hamish's highland radar picked up something from Jimmy's brain that was nothing to do with a craving for drink. He turned round and stared at him.

'Piss off!' snarled Jimmy.

Hamish walked back and sat down again. 'You're shifty and guilty. You've always been an honest man, Jimmy, but something is telling me you've been lying.'

'Of course I've been lying,' howled Jimmy. 'We've all been lying.'

Hamish sent up a prayer. Forgive me for what I am

about to do. Aloud he said, 'There are other pubs, you know. I mean, you're supposed to be having time off.'

Jimmy sighed. 'I was sitting here, hoping the powers-that-be would think kindly of me. At the moment, I'm down in their minds as a useless drunk. Man, I feel ill.'

'Come on,' said Hamish. 'I'll buy you a dram.'

They walked to a pub near Jimmy's flat. All through Britain now there are smart pubs with restaurants, all trying to tempt back the customers who were driven away by the smoking ban. But Jimmy's local, The Grand Mackay, was grimy and sleazy – though with one great asset. You walked down a short corridor from the main bar into a room with air extractors strong enough to tear the hair from your head.

It was packed with small, smelly men, shouting into each other's faces. Hamish urged Jimmy back out. 'You never smoke much,' he complained.

'No, but I wanted one wee sook for old times' sake. Oh, well, get me a double Grouse.'

Hamish secured a table in a corner and then came back with the whisky for Jimmy and a tonic water for himself.

'I'm not drinking alone,' snarled Jimmy.

'I'll get the barman to put a gin in it,' said Hamish. He loathed gin but decided that any sacrifice to get Jimmy talking was worth it.

Settled at the table once more, Hamish noticed Jimmy's face relaxing as he downed a double whisky. He had taken the precaution of bringing him another one.

'Jimmy, was there any investigation into those builders from Invergordon?'

'Aye. Regular.'

'Go yourself?'

'No, Blair went wi' a couple o' sidekicks.'

'I might go and have a look at them myself.'

'Oh, stop stirring things up, Hamish. It's all swept under the carpet.'

'Did you actually hear Handy confessing to the murder?'

'No, but that new copper, Karl Strith, heard him and told Daviot, who then swore he'd heard him as well.'

'Right,' said Hamish. 'Let's get you home.'

'Just leave me.'

'This may seem awfy strange, Jimmy, but I like you and I don't want to see you getting a wet brain. Come on, man, or I'll put the cuffs on you.'

Hamish escorted him to his flat. He was surprised it was so neat and clean.

He walked back to the police Land Rover where two pairs of eyes looked at him accusingly. 'Sorry,' said Hamish, hugging his pets. 'I forgot you. But I think I'll never see Sonsie again and I think a damn murderer is still around, running free, and I am not going to get any help.'

But help was to come from somewhere he did not expect.

Chapter Ten

The best laid schemes o' mice an' men
Gang aft a-gley.

—Robert Burns

Harriet Munro strolled along the Beauly road in Inverness a week later. The day was fine, everything sparkling in the late spring sunshine. She was enjoying a new freedom in her own little flat away from the carping voice of her father. Harriet was on her way to visit her aunt Agnes.

Agnes Munro had never married. She was very tall with a large bosom and a big nose. She looked like a figurehead on a ship. She had been a schoolteacher but had taken early retirement. She was delighted to see her niece and plied her with tea and cakes. Harriet refused the cakes. 'I'm on a diet.' She leaned forward and said, 'You always said looks don't matter.'

'That was a bit stupid,' said Agnes. 'I think men don't matter. Careers last. Men don't.'

Harriet sat silent, staring at the floor. Agnes looked at that unfortunate little moustache. 'Are you a virgin, Harriet?'

'No. Why do you ask?' demanded Harriet. 'Are virgins hairy?'

'Yes, well, some o' the time. Tell you what. There's this Bosnian woman, Sonia, who has set up a wee place two doors away. She can clean up your face and eyebrows. Lassie, you've got lovely eyes. Did no one ever tell you that?'

'A policeman did.'

'Come on. This is exciting.'

Had Sonia been a hard-faced sophisticated blonde, or something similar, Harriet would have backed out of the shop, but she turned out to be a grey-haired woman in her seventies with a motherly face.

Harriet emerged some time later, blinking in the sunlight. Her aunt was almost skipping along the pavement. 'You look a different person altogether. Now, clothes!'

'I've plenty o' clothes, Auntie.'

'What you've got on is baggy and shapeless. Let's go!'

There was no *Pretty Woman* or Cinderella moment for Harriet when she arrived at work. She was just Harriet to the staff but something different.

When they did notice was when the new European sales rep, Monsieur Pierre Duval, came into the offices.

He was fortyish with thick curly black hair, a tall, rangy body, a smile, and oh, that French accent. And the boss was busy and asked Harriet Munro to take this pagan god for lunch.

'What's happened to Hairy Harriet?' hissed a filing clerk. 'Why does she get to take him to lunch?'

But Harriet had one great seductive talent – she was a good listener. After she had given Pierre a succinct description of the firm's business in Scotland, she asked him about himself. He talked about the firms he had worked for, said he was originally from the Auvergne region of France but had mostly worked in Paris. His wife had left him for another man and he had no children.

'But you wear a wedding ring,' said Harriet.

'I am only telling you about the divorce. If I tell the ladies, they can get the wrong idea.'

'And I am not a lady?' said Harriet.

'You are my confessor. I haven't talked this much in a long time. I look into those beautiful eyes of yours and I open my big mouth and yakkity-yakk.'

'You'll get a warm welcome in Scotland,' said Harriet. 'We have strong historical ties with France.'

'Then why do people hate us so much?'

'What are you talking about?'

'This is really the country of John Knox, is it not? I have been called a papist, as if it is something dirty.'

'Oh, dear,' said Harriet. 'Pay no heed. There are so many bigots around. It's said people will kill for love, but look at all the fanatics who kill over religion. I have a certain sympathy with that professor who was murdered. Get rid of religion and God. But he was too passionate. Gosh, there must have been a lot who could . . .'

'What is it?'

Harriet shook her head. 'An idea. I'll need to think about it.'

Spring moved into summer and Hamish had almost forgotten the murders. They hung around somewhere at the back of his mind, but crime was nearly nonexistent, the days were warm and sunny, and he spent long hours fishing with his two dogs playing in the heather.

And then one Sunday when he was returning to the station, he saw a small woman he did not at first recognize. It was only when he drew nearer and saw those eyes that he realized it was a transformed Harriet Munro.

'Miss Munro! What brings you? Nothing up, I hope?'

'May we go? I've been turning this theory over in my mind. Probably daft.'

'Come ben,' urged Hamish, marvelling at her new appearance. In the kitchen, he pulled out a seat for her at the table.

'Coffee?'

'Yes, please. Black, no sugar.'

Hamish sat down opposite her. He noticed a diamond ring on her engagement finger.

'Who's the happy man?' he asked.

'A French sales rep. But he's got a job in Lyon and we're moving there. I want to be away from my father. I don't want to be crushed again, although it'll never quite go away. Somewhere down inside me, I'll always be Hairy Harriet.'

'Have you heard from Martha?'

'Not recently. She used to be on the phone the whole time. Selwyn had got her pregnant. She got an abortion and a new job. She's personal assistant to the assistant manager of Homeland Gin.'

'And is that what you came to tell me?'

'No. I came to talk about religion. You would think with ISIS and all that, that there would be fear and hatred of the Muslim community, but it is the hatred between the Protestants and Catholics that runs deep. So I remembered what you said. All of it. About the minister preaching the Song of Solomon in the kirk when Olivia was there; about the minister's sister having a crush on Selwyn. So I got to thinking, what if Sheila was desperately in love with Selwyn? And what if the manipulative Olivia thought it would be fun to get the professor and Peter Haggis together and see what happened? Sheila sees her brother losing not only his heart but his faith. Selwyn couldn't keep it in his trousers and so he led Sheila to believe that if Olivia were out of the way, he would marry her. I think she might have killed him. I think before that, she followed the professor when he left the manse one evening. I don't think the wails in the tower scared her one bit. Maybe she coaxed him up there, claiming to be

192

frightened. Such a man as Professor Gordon would pooh-pooh all supernatural manifestations. Maybe she pushed him. Maybe he just fell into the hole under the leaves and broke his own neck. Maybe I'm talking rubbish. I mean, it's nothing to do with Catholics versus Protestants. It's just that religion in Scotland can rouse black and dangerous feelings. It could be the minister feeling that Professor Gordon was trying to destroy his faith or perhaps Sheila, worried about her brother, passionate about Selwyn, and hating Olivia.'

'You've given me a lot to think about,' said Hamish.

'Maybe I've got it all wrong and it's nothing to do with a woman at all. I'm anti my own sex at the moment.'

'Why?'

'When I was Hairy Harriet, the women in the office were so friendly, always wanting help with computer stuff and so on. Ever since I got engaged, they skulk in corners and glare at me.'

'You'll soon be shot of them so don't worry.'

'That's not really what is bothering me.'

'So what is worrying you?'

'Do I really love Pierre or is it because everyone else seems to think he's such a glamorous catch?'

'I'm sure you do,' said Hamish. He wanted to say that if you were in love, you had no doubts about it. But then, he had met happily married couples who knew love but not the highs of romantic passion.

When she had gone, he realized it was Sunday. He phoned up Jock at the store in Drim and found there

193

was to be an evening service. Before he set out, he drove to Braikie to see how Alice Douglas was getting on. Handy's sister had agreed to continue paying rent on the villa.

He was relieved to find Alice Douglas at home and looking happy and well. Hamish had been afraid he might find her husband back again or that he had been replaced by another brute, such had been his previous experience of battered wives. He refused tea, only pleased to see that for Alice, the nightmare was over. Her divorce would be final in late summer.

When he left, he found there was still time for him to visit Dick and Anka. But he had to admit to himself he was jealous of Dick. I'm no better than Harriet's office women, he thought. But he went on up into the moors and let the dogs out to play in the heather.

Maybe he was chasing after idiotic solutions, he thought. He lay in the bell heather with his hands behind his head and watched two buzzards sailing up against a pale-blue sky.

There had been enough drugs in Handy's possession to drive men to kill. The gang pretending to be builders could easily have done the murders on Handy's orders. The genuine company in Invergordon had said that Handy had employed them, but failed to say until later that he had paid them off some weeks before Hamish had first met Handy. Perhaps the professor, Olivia, and Selwyn had somehow just got in the way.

At last, he rose and whistled to Lugs and Sally and headed off through the calm evening to Drim.

He was late and as he parked the Land Rover, he could hear the strains of the opening hymn, 'Abide with Me', floating out on the evening air. He slipped into a pew at the back of the church. Peter Haggis looked remarkably tame and ordinary, far from the impassioned man who had read from the Song of Solomon. He seemed to be going through the motions of conducting the service. He intoned a sermon on God's forgiveness, saying the piece about there being more rejoicing in heaven over the arrival of a sinner than of one righteous man.

Hamish studied the backs of the heads in front of him. He recognized some of the crofters and their wives and Jock and Ailsa and Edie Aubrey.

Drim had always been a secretive place. Someone had once put forward the view that people who lived at the end of valleys were more withdrawn and superstitious than people who lived in the open plains. Had all those crossed branches at their doors been meant to ward off a real and present danger rather than a ghostly one?

He shook his head. No, that couldn't be right. Threaten a highlander? Jock and his neighbours would have descended on those supposed builders with their shotguns at the ready.

Why couldn't he just relax? As Handy had proved to be that most hated thing in Hamish's mind, a corrupt police officer, then it stood to reason that a few murders wouldn't bother him. He possibly didn't even have to do them himself. Just order one of the gang to do it for him.

But he sensed badness in the church caused by fear.

After the service, Hamish decided to go to the builders in Invergordon the next day. If he even got a scent of villainy from them, he could leave suspecting anyone in Drim alone.

They had been investigated already but he wanted to see the firm for himself.

Charlie said he would come with him. They decided to find a café somewhere for lunch because both were feeling guilty at relying on the hotel's picnic hampers.

'It's all Polish food now,' said Hamish. 'My mother remembers when it was the Italians. Not that they served spaghetti in the cafés. Pie and peas, fish and chips, burgers and snacks, but they were so clean compared with the old flyblown dumps.'

'I like Polish places,' said Charlie dreamily. 'Polish lassies hae these cheekbones. I like a lassie wi' high cheekbones. I like the food as well.'

Invergordon, on the east coast, is a town known for repairing oil rigs on the Cromarty Firth. It is sometimes known as Little Glasgow, because that's where so many of the workers came from.

The builders' yard was situated on the waterfront. As they drove up outside, Hamish noticed that it looked like a regular family business.

At first he got a sour welcome from a man, Strachan Mackenzie, who said he was part owner. 'I've had enough o' you lot. Had to complain to the chief constable.'

'That would not have been because of a Detective Chief Inspector Blair?' asked Hamish.

'Aye, that's the bullying bastard. Get the hell out o' here!'

Hamish smiled. 'Now, I am not bullying you, am I?'

'No, but . . .'

'I am not accusing you of anything at all. I only wondered when your men had stopped working for Ebrington Handy over at Drim. See? A simple little question. You answer it, and we'll go away.'

'Oh, well,' he said in a mollified tone. 'I ken it fine. He pulled the crew off last December. One o' my men went ower and saw a squad working and I phoned him about it. He said he'd got a cheaper builder, so that was that.'

'Now, see how easy that was,' said Hamish. 'We're off.'

'I wonder why Blair thought it necessary to go for him?' said Charlie as they got back into the Land Rover.

'It was probably a few minutes before opening time,' said Hamish, 'and the idiot craved a drink. There's a place here, I mind, called The Purple Turtle. Good burgers.'

They each had a large lunch, so large that Hamish could feel all his worries about the murders slowly fading away. Harriet Munro was a very forceful personality. Perhaps he should take this opportunity of going back to the lazy life in Lochdubh he loved so much.

By the time he dropped Charlie off and cruised slowly down into Lochdubh and saw the village lying by the calm loch, he decided that life was too short. Why fight it?

But why had Blair not investigated further, once he found out that the real workers had been laid off?

As he climbed down from the Land Rover and let the dogs out, he turned and saw Heather Lomond, standing by the kitchen door.

'What is it now?' asked Hamish wearily.

She threw back her head and placed a hand on her bosom. 'I have a boyfriend!'

'Many happy returns,' said Hamish. 'Stand aside.'

'So I just want you to know, I don't need you.'

'That's grand, Heather. Good night!'

Hamish strode past her, let himself in, and slammed the door. He wondered whether Mrs Wellington realized that her niece was a fantasist. Did she really have a boyfriend? Or had some hiker stopped to ask for directions and smiled at her?

He filled the dogs' water bowls. Reminding them sharply that he had fed them hamburgers, he strolled into the living room and sank down on the battered sofa.

Women! He'd never understand them. But Harriet Munro certainly would. She had not thought that the idea the murderer might be a woman too far-fetched.

Could it have been Handy's sister after all? Could she really not have known where the money came from? Or what about Sheila Haggis with the haunted, passionate eyes?

He contemplated visiting Sheila the next day and trying to get some suspicious reaction out of her. But he had

198

been looking forward to a day's fishing on the river with the colonel and Charlie.

Before he fell asleep, he suddenly remembered Martha Dundas. She had been made pregnant. She'd had an abortion. But he could picture her breaking down and sobbing. Not having the passion-fuelled rage necessary to kill a man. What had the autopsy on Selwyn found? He had been struck on the head with a blunt instrument.

Hamish tossed and turned for most of the night. By morning, he had decided that he must investigate only a little further to get any peace of mind. He phoned Charlie and said he would not be fishing. He checked his bank balance. Not bad. He had won first prize for hill racing at the last Highland Games. Forget Drim for the day. He would fly down to Glasgow and see if he could find out anything from Freda.

Hamish was always amazed that a city like Glasgow which could produce some of the warmest, kindest, and funniest people on the planet should yet give birth to someone like Blair. He arrived in the late afternoon and took a taxi to Freda's home.

Freda turned out to live in a mews house at the back of one of the Victorian terraces in the West End. Although it was small, Hamish reckoned it would cost a lot, around four hundred thousand. He suddenly wished he had phoned in advance. Maybe she had found a job.

He rang the bell. A seagull suddenly screamed over-head, staring down at him as if demanding to know what he was doing so far from Lochdubh. The door suddenly opened and Freda stood there, wrapped in an old-fashioned camel-hair dressing gown.

'I'm right sorry to wake you . . .' began Hamish.

'You didn't. I was having a siesta. Come in.'

The front door led straight into a living room, which, Hamish guessed, would have been the carriage house when it was built. He could never understand the fashion for mews houses. They had been built for coach-men out of cheap brick and were usually north facing.

The living room was cold and dark, shadowed as it was by a large wall outside the window on the other side of the narrow lane.

Hamish looked around. There were no expensive items. The furniture seemed to be of the cheapest kind. There were no books or pictures, just a large television screen on one wall. The three-piece suite was uphol-stered in brown corduroy. The coffee table in front of it was of the flat-pack kind.

'So sit down and tell me what brings you,' said Freda.

'I am just curious,' said Hamish. 'You see, I cannot believe your brother murdered anyone. But he may have ordered one of his gang to do the killing.'

She shook her head. 'Now, look, is this official?'

'No. And I don't want the police to know I've been here.'

'Well, in return for signing a lot of papers swearing me to secrecy, I had to agree that my brother was a serial killer so they could secretly close the case while giving him an honourable burial. I agreed in return for this place, a payoff, and goodbye. But Handy phoned me before he fled to the airport. He told me he had never killed anyone though he had been dealing drugs. I felt sick. I swear to God, I thought the money came from the sale of Lady Jane.

'Did you know he was very religious?'

'Handy!' exclaimed Hamish. 'I cannae believe it.'

'Oh, believe it. You see, to him drugs were just another form of alcohol. He swore cannabis was safer than booze any day.'

'So you did know about it?'

'He talked to me on the phone all the way to the airport. It was the first I'd heard of it. I think it all began when his last marriage fell through. She was a nasty little gold digger and she dumped him for some rich villain over on Clydebank. I think he went a bit off his trolley after that.'

'He may have taken agin that professor for his anti-God preaching,' said Hamish.

'I don't think so. If Professor Gordon had called, I'd have seen him, I'm sure of that. Look, are you sure no one must know you are here?'

'I would lose my job.'

'Then why don't I take you out for dinner? Forget about the damn case. Or maybe I'll get drunk and remember something useful.'

'Well, maybe somewhere not too expensive,' said Hamish.

'Oh, I can afford it. Wait till I change.'

'What about me?' protested Hamish, who was in civilian clothes. 'I don't have a tie.'

'You've got a white shirt and tweed jacket on. I've got a tie somewhere. The last one-night stand left it. Help yourself to a drink. In the kitchen.'

Hamish wandered into the kitchen. He opened the cupboards. He found one cupboard full of medicine bottles and packets. He noticed packets of amphetamines. His eyes narrowed. The only way she could have got that amount was illegally. He poured himself a small whisky from a bottle in another cupboard and then sat down in the living room to wait.

Freda eventually appeared wearing a leopard-skin-patterned blouse, tight jeans, and stilettos. She handed Hamish a tie.

'Before we go out,' said Hamish, 'you've got a supply of drugs in the kitchen. Did your brother get them for you?'

'No. You're sure you are not here officially?'

'I swear.'

'I got them through Maggie's.'

'Could you do me a favour,' pleaded Hamish. 'Don't take any afore we go out. I cannae bear folk on uppers. They chatter, chatter, chatter and think they're being so witty when they're boring for Britain.'

'Bitch, that's what you are. Oh, let's go.' She swung a white mohair stole around her shoulders.

* * *

They dined at Seafood Lux, a fish restaurant in the centre of Glasgow. Hamish would have enjoyed a plate of lobster Newburg immensely if it had not transpired that Freda must have had some uppers cached somewhere else and taken them before leaving the mews. She gabbled on and on about what a bastard her late husband had been and how he used to beat her up. I wonder if he ever punched her in the mouth, wondered Hamish, watching the thin red lips opposite pour out venom. He fantasized having a roll of duct tape, tearing off a strip, and shutting her up so that he could enjoy his food.

There is nothing more infuriatingly sad, he thought, than the type of woman who wears leopard-print clothes, takes uppers, and decides she is utterly fascinating. She had ordered a bottle of Nuits-Saint-Georges, cackling, 'So it's red, so what?' She glugged most of it, actually glugged, thought Hamish. He could hear it going down her gullet, glug, glug, glug.

A large man suddenly loomed over their table. 'Evening, Freda,' he said. 'Who's your fella?'

'This is—'

'Donald Gordon,' said Hamish quickly.

'And how did you two meet?' the big man asked.

'Don't I get an introduction?' asked Hamish.

'My name is Barry Wilkinson, for my sins.'

Hamish had a sudden, malicious desire to annoy. 'What have your sins got to do with it?'

'Oh, just a way of speaking. Where did you two meet?'

Hamish rose to his considerable height. 'Push off,' he said. 'You are spoiling my evening.'

Barry turned bright red but muttered, 'I'll be waiting for you.'

When he had left, Freda said, 'Oh, Lord. That was one of my ex's best friends.'

But the visit from Barry had calmed her down. Freda suddenly said she did not want dessert or coffee, she wanted to go home.

Hamish told the waiter to call a taxi. He escorted Freda to the door of the restaurant but did not go outside with her, only bidding her a firm farewell. Then he walked back in and asked if he could use a back or side entrance, tipping the waiter heavily.

The waiter led him through the kitchens and out into a lane at the back. Hamish cautiously circled round and looked at the front of the restaurant. Barry was standing there with two evil-looking thugs. Hamish retreated back down the lane, which joined another one and so allowed him to make his way out and round to Buchanan Street Bus Station where he caught a bus to the airport. He slept in the airport on a hard chair and woke up wondering if any of his journey had been of any use at all.

Hamish was often to think that if it hadn't been for the midges, those Scottish mosquitoes, the murderer might have got away.

He woke the next morning and, as he fried bacon for

breakfast, he experienced a feeling of relief. Once more, it was a sunny day. Why should he worry and fret? He collected his fishing rod and tackle and set out with his dogs for the Tommel Castle Hotel. Charlie was delighted to see him, but the colonel was not and was apt to sulk.

It was when they were out on the river that black clouds of midges descended on them and not one of them had remembered to bring any repellent. They packed up and fled back to the castle and the comfort of antihistamine cream.

Hamish then drove back to the station. The day had turned muggy, a milky colour, and the loch was still and flat. A seal cut a V through the placid water. It rolled on its side and appeared to stare straight at Hamish. He gave a superstitious shudder. The highlander believes that people come back as seals.

Hamish had a sudden impulse to talk to the police-man Karl Strith, the one who had claimed to have heard Handy confessing to the murder of Selwyn. He decided to ask Angela to keep an eye on his dogs and then wondered why he had not thought of talking to her again instead of going all the way to Tain to take Harriet out for dinner. He realized uneasily that even with her hairy appearance, there had been something almost magnetic about Harriet, and a strong earthy sexuality.

'My mind's in my balls,' he said to Lugs as he walked along the waterfront in the direction of Angela's cottage.

'Did you hear that!' A shrill voice right behind him made him jump. He swung round. There stood the Currie sisters, eyes accusing.

'I am not going to explain,' yelled Hamish. 'Run along. Shoo!'

'Lecher!' howled Nessie and her echo said, 'Lecher', but in a plaintive wail.

Is everyone mad? wondered Hamish as he dived thankfully in the open door of Angela's cottage. If I don't disappear somewhere for the day, they'll all be round at the police station, the monstrous regiment of women, staring and accusing and claiming I've broken Heather's heart or something.

Angela said she would take care of the dogs, unless they dared to bark at her cats, in which case she would lock them in the station.

Hamish had called at the hotel to borrow Charlie's car, not wanting the police Land Rover to be noticed in Strathbane. He parked several streets away from the station and phoned Jimmy, saying he wanted to talk to him in private. To his surprise, Jimmy told him he would see him at Jo's Café in the High Street instead of choosing a pub.

Hamish was even more surprised to find a healthy-looking Jimmy marching into the café.

'You look great,' he said. 'Off the booze?'

'Aye, for a bit until my liver gets a rest. There's this new nurse at headquarters, Shona Sutherland. Man, blonde hair and legs up to her armpits. I'll get a date out of her yet. So what do you want?'

'I want a quiet word with Karl Strith.'

'He's gone. Left the force.'

'So where is he now?'

'I don't know!' said Jimmy, looking exasperated. 'Look, thanks to you, I am Strathbane's golden child. Don't rock the boat. It's all swept under the carpet. Forget it.'

'Okay. Why did this Karl leave the force?'

'I don't know,' said Jimmy, moodily stirring the froth on his cappuccino.

'Yes, you do.'

Jimmy jumped to his feet. 'Sod you! I'm out of here.'

Hamish gazed after him. Someone must know where Karl had gone. But Strith was an odd name. He paid for the coffee and walked back to the car where he looked through the local phone directory on his iPad. No K. Strith, but a J. Strith was listed on Rannoch Crescent off the Lochinver road.

Hamish drove to the address and knocked at the door of a trim bungalow. A woman with hair dyed so blonde it was nearly white answered the door.

'Does Karl live here?' asked Hamish.

'I'm his mother. Why do you want him?'

'Just a wee chat for old times' sake. I was on the force with him.'

'You'll find him at the mall in the centre o' town. He's one of the security guards.'

Hamish drove off again. A greasy drizzle was smearing the windscreen. Normally an unambitious contented man, Hamish felt upset and uneasy. It was all very well for Jimmy and his like to sweep everything under the carpet, but he could not rest easy thinking there was a murderer on the loose.

He parked in the mall's multistorey and then walked through the mall, looking to left and right for the security guard.

Outside a computer shop, he saw a tall, thin young man in a security guard's uniform. Hamish approached him. 'Karl Strith?'

'Yeah, that's me. Who are you?' Hamish was not in uniform.

Hamish introduced himself. Karl had pale-grey eyes. They suddenly looked like sea-washed glass. 'What d'ye want?' he demanded.

'A wee talk about Handy's confession.'

Karl stared at him for a long moment and then asked, 'Who sent you?'

'Relax. No one knows I am here. Let's go to that coffee shop over there.'

Karl shuffled his feet. He was still wearing his old regulation boots. Then he glanced at his watch.

'Okay. It's nearly ma break.'

In the coffee shop, Karl ordered hot chocolate with marshmallows on top and Hamish had a black coffee. 'Who's paying?' demanded Karl.

'I am.'

Karl promptly put three iced doughnuts on a plate and took them with his coffee to a table, leaving Hamish to pay the bill.

'So,' said Hamish, 'what gave you the idea that Handy confessed to murdering Selwyn Sinclair?'

208

'Because I heard him.'

'You've got icing sugar all down your tunic,' said Hamish. 'Now, here's what is happening. I think I know who the real murderer is and I'm going to expose that person, which will show you up as a liar. What do you think of that?'

Karl had fair eyelashes which blinked rapidly. 'But he did say it. Detective Chief Inspector Blair heard it.'

'Oh, aye. But I swear you didn't.'

'Look, this is what happened. Blair tells me that Handy whispered the confession, right?'

'Okay.'

'He says to me, he says, "I'll let you take the credit, laddie." Well, Blair's the big cheese, so I fair jumped at the chance.'

'So why did you leave the force?'

'Well, see, Blair takes me aside and says it's all got to be hush-hush and they'd find I'd been lying. He said he could get me this job, and man I jumped at it. Better pay and regular hours.'

'Karl, you've cleared my mind,' said Hamish. 'We won't talk any more about it.'

Chapter Eleven

When the Hymalayan peasant meets the he-bear
  in his pride,
He shouts to scare the monster, who will often
  turn aside.
But the she-bear thus accosted rends the peasant
  tooth and nail,
For the female of the species is more deadly than
  the male.

—Rudyard Kipling

Hamish drove slowly and thoughtfully to Drim. He wanted to visit the manse and sniff the air, put out the tentacles of his highland radar, and see if he could pick up anything.

If he sensed everything was all right, he might drive to Tain and find Martha. Selwyn had got her pregnant. She was the one who had found his body. Why not just get the police to check up on him? *Because she was pregnant*, said a voice in his brain, *and probably desperate*.

210

As he drove down into Drim, a little round black cloud blotted out the sun, sending a shadow lying across the manse.

If I ever get this cleared up, he thought, I never ever want to come here again. I hate this place.

He rang the bell. Silence. A puff of wind sent angry little waves coursing down the loch, a seagull screamed and dived, and then silence fell again.

Hamish retreated to Jock's shop. Ailsa was behind the counter. 'Seen the minister?' asked Hamish.

'Havenae seen himself the day,' said Ailsa. 'Want a pie? Got some fresh.'

'No. Wait! Are those Anka's baps there?'

'Aye, get a big delivery every week from Braikie. They're all right even though they've been frozen.'

Hamish realized he was hungry. 'What about a bacon bap, Ailsa?'

'Sure. Coming up. Want a beer?'

'I'm driving.'

'You cannae arrest yourself and one won't put you ower the limit.'

'Fine, Ailsa, that would be grand. Did you know about anyone peddling drugs around here?'

'No, not even a bit o' pot.'

'What about uppers?'

'No such luck. I'm that tired these days, I could dae with something.'

When Hamish's food was ready he took it outside to a small table along with a bottle of beer.

He looked across the curve of the loch's bay towards the manse. Perhaps there would be an evening service. Surely Haggis must return to prepare for that. He was just finishing his bap and the last dregs of beer when he felt there was something out of place, something that had caught the corner of his eye. It had been over in the direction of the manse and the round church.

There it was!

There was a flicker of light across a narrow window of the church and then it had gone again.

He got up and got rid of his trash before striding off in the direction of the church. When he got to the main door, he tried the handle, but the door was locked. He was about to knock when he had a sudden desire to see what was going on inside in secret.

He walked round the side of the church, through the Celtic crosses on the graveyard to a side door. It was locked as well. But it was a simple Yale lock. He took out a thin strip of metal he kept for cases such as this and sprang the lock.

He found himself in what he gathered was the vestry.

Hamish gently opened the door into the main body of the church.

He stiffened as he heard a familiar voice.

'You see I am a good judge of character,' the voice was saying, 'and Macbeth will never give up. So you pair are going to take the rap. You, Sheila, have that typed confession in front of you. Sign it and you and your brother will have a quick, nearly painless death. Don't sign and it'll be hell on earth.'

212

Hamish edged forward.

Harriet Munro was standing with her back to him, holding a wicked-looking black revolver.

'As God is my witness, we will never, either of us, sign such lies. Do your worst and may God have mercy on your soul,' said Peter Haggis.

Hamish was glad that brother and sister had tape over their eyes, otherwise they might have seen him and alerted Harriet.

He eased up to the altar and seized a plain brass cross.

'Let's see how long you can last,' jeered Harriet. 'We'll start with your kneecaps, Sheila.'

'Why are you doing this?' wailed Sheila.

'I told you. Sign that or bang go your kneecaps.'

'No!'

'Very well.'

Hamish threw the brass cross. It caught Harriet on the back of the neck and she dropped like a stone. I hope I havenae killed her, thought Hamish. I couldnae stand the paperwork.

He went up and felt for a pulse. She was unconscious but the pulse was quite strong.

He tore the tape from Peter and Sheila's eyes and mouths. Both had wet themselves with fear and Sheila was as white as clay. Hamish phoned for an ambulance and then spoke to headquarters.

He eased the revolver from Harriet's hand. It was a Modele 1892 revolver, standard issue to officers in the First World War. He wondered if it belonged to her fiancé: perhaps a family souvenir. A roll of duct tape that

Harriet had used to bind her prisoners lay beside Sheila's chair. Hamish picked it up and used it to secure Harriet's wrists and ankles.

'Go into the manse, Mr Haggis,' he said. 'You'll feel better when you clean yourselves up.'

Sheila tried to stand up but her knees buckled under her. 'On second thoughts,' said Hamish, 'leave her be for the moment. Do you have anything to make tea with in the kirk?'

'There's a wee kitchen next to the vestry.'

'Right. A cup of tea with a lot of sugar.'

Peter's eyes burned with passion. 'I prayed to the Lord to save us, and he heard my prayer. I will never doubt again.'

'Great,' said Hamish sourly. 'Make the tea.'

If he pointed out that it was a very human Hamish Macbeth who had saved them, then, he was sure, all Peter would do was call him an instrument of God.

Hamish soaked a handkerchief in the font and knelt down beside Harriet and bathed her forehead. Peter came back with a cup of tea. But Sheila moaned that she wanted to go home and this time was able to stand.

Harriet's eyes suddenly flew open. For a brief moment, they looked puzzled and then slowly filled with hate. She rolled over on her side.

'Tell me about it, Harriet,' coaxed Hamish. He drew out a powerful little tape recorder and placed it on the floor. 'It's just you and me, Harriet. Why?'

'I loved him,' she said. 'He said he'd marry me if he could get rid of Olivia so I did it for him. And then

214

droopy Martha corners me in the ladies and starts to cry, saying she's pregnant and he won't marry her. So Selwyn was such a bastard, I knew I'd never live a quiet moment while he was on this earth. I called at his home late. Said something important in business had come up. They had one of those glass rolling pins in the kitchen and so when his back was turned, getting me a drink, I biffed him hard.'

'And what about the professor?'

She sighed. 'I used to meet Selwyn in the tower. We didn't for a minute believe in ghosts and it was one way of making sure no one would disturb us. I went to meet him and there's this prof poking about. He said he had come to talk to the minister but had decided to inspect the ruin instead. He wouldn't go away. I was exasperated. I gave him an almighty push, and imagine my amazement when he staggered back and fell through the floor. When Selwyn arrived, I persuaded him a hotel room would be a better bet and off we went. But I was frightened the body would begin to smell. I forced myself to go down there one night. I found his car keys. He had left his car up at the entrance to the village. I drove it up on a bluff and then sent it down into the loch. Then I got that old wheelbarrow from outside Jock's. I knew about that passage. I smashed the locks and put other padlocks in their place. I wheeled the body down to the loch and pushed it in. It gets deep quick and the tide was going out and it took him away.'

With a feeling of relief, Hamish heard approaching

215

sirens. 'Why me?' he asked. 'Why go out for dinner with me and encourage me to go on hunting?'

'Because I knew you would never give up, that you would get round to me in the end. I saw it in here.' She tapped her forehead and stared at him with those wide, wide eyes and for a moment, he experienced a shudder of fear.

'But what a waste!' said Hamish. 'Everything was coming right for you.'

'Too late. Imagine what it was like. But there were a couple of times when Martha couldn't go on trips with him and he took me. He made me feel beautiful.'

The sirens wailed like so many banshees, heralding death. Hamish's phone call had exploded at head-quarters and a full contingent headed by Daviot arrived.

Hamish formally told Harriet she was being arrested for the murders of Olivia and Selwyn Sinclair.

When Daviot walked in and demanded a report, Hamish stood to attention and delivered it and remarked he had also got it on tape.

'Why couldn't you have left well alone!' shouted Daviot, and then turned red with embarrassment as Hamish stared at him. 'I mean, well done, Macbeth.'

Blair lumbered forward looking worried. 'Are ye sure, Macbeth, that this wee lassie did those murders?'

'Miss Munro has confessed. When I arrived, as I have just reported, she was threatening to shoot Sheila Haggis in the kneecaps if she did not confess to the murder.'

Daviot summoned two policewomen to take the prisoner to Strathbane. Jimmy Anderson and Detective

216

Andy MacNab said they would follow and begin the interrogation. The forensic team moved in and Hamish, Daviot, Blair, and a detective constable called Henry Fox moved to the manse.

'I've phoned the doctor,' said the minister. 'We are both in shock.'

'I see Miss Haggis has already taken something,' said Hamish, looking at Sheila's washed-out dreamy face.

'We have some Valium. I admit she may have taken too many.'

Daviot introduced everyone and explained he would send a car for them in the morning so that they could make their official statements at police headquarters.

'But in the meantime,' said Daviot, avoiding looking at Hamish, 'Detective Fox here will take your preliminary statements. Macbeth, there is no need for you to stay.'

'Don't be ridiculous,' said Peter waspishly. 'That sergeant saved our lives. He is part of our statement.'

'Yes, yes,' said Daviot fussily. 'You may stay, Macbeth.'

'I think I can take the statements here,' said Fox. 'I have my computer and travelling printer with me.'

'Oh, good man!' exclaimed Daviot.

Hamish intercepted the wary, calculating look Blair threw at Fox. Good. As long as the detective chief inspector had someone else to worry about, it suited Hamish very well.

At last it was over. Sheila and Peter Haggis signed their statements and were told that someone from Victim Support would be arriving.

'That was efficient, Fox,' said Daviot.

'I follow your example at all times, sir,' said Fox.

Oh, dear, thought Hamish. Now Blair is really worried. Fox is not only clever but a sycophant as well. For that was why Daviot kept Blair close. He was a weak man. Unsure of his position and with a domineering wife, he relied on Blair to boost his ego.

But Fox was young and clever with a pleasant face and a lilting Irish accent. He knew Daviot would immediately lean on him because there would be mountains of paperwork. At least Handy hadn't been a murderer. Unless you considered supplying drugs as mass murder. Perhaps people who planted the seeds of death should take the rap as well. What about Harriet's jeering father? And Handy polluting the Highlands with dangerous drugs?

It could be argued that Selwyn and Olivia with all their seductions and manipulations brought about their own murders.

'So she murdered the professor as well,' he realized Peter was saying.

'No, I think she was telling the truth when she said he fell through the floor and broke his neck. He had been seen with Olivia Sinclair.'

'I feel that may have been my fault,' moaned Peter. 'I told Olivia about the hauntings at the tower and she said she would introduce me to the professor who didn't believe in God and would knock some sense into me. I loved Olivia and she laughed at my faith, may God

218

forgive her. But thanks to God's messenger, Sergeant Macbeth, I do believe.'

He fell to his knees and began to pray while the forces of law and order stood around him and shuffled their feet with the exception of Fox, who was studying Hamish. He had heard whispers that it was really Hamish who solved crimes and let other people take the credit because he didn't want promotion. He would get close to Hamish and study his methods. And then he realized Hamish was looking at him and giving an infinitesimal shake of his head. He looked down quickly. He felt uneasily that Hamish had just read his mind.

Blair wished someone would stop the praying minister so they could all leave. He was worried sick. Strith would need to keep his mouth shut and not tell anyone it was he, Blair, who had claimed to have heard Handy confessing to the murder of Selwyn. All the Big Yins, the Suits, would be back with their endless questions and demands for quotes in triplicate. The young smugglers would walk free of any charge. Why had he done it? He would not admit that he was jealous of Handy and it was because Handy had treated him with contempt. He began to fret. He could not possibly leave until forensics had finished with the church, and then he and the others would be expected to examine it. Waste of time, he fretted. Macbeth had it all sewn up, the bastard. And that crawling wee creep Fox was a danger. He had even joined the lodge. Like Jimmy, he had temporarily stopped drinking alcohol, and now he craved a dram with terrible ferocity.

And then he felt a gentle tug at his sleeve. It was Henry Fox, his guileless blue eyes looking into Blair's tortured ones. 'Would you be liking a wee dram, sir?' he whispered. 'I have a flask.'

For one brief moment, Blair's face lit up, but then it closed down and he snapped, 'No drinking on duty.'

Fox stepped back and nearly collided with the tall figure of Hamish Macbeth, who said out of the side of his mouth, 'That's no' the way to get his job, you manipulating sod.'

But the devil was on Fox's side because Peter had long finished praying and had left the room, only to return with a bottle of fine malt whisky and a tray of glasses.

'I was keeping this for Hogmanay,' he said, 'but this is a special occasion. The Good Lord chose to send his angel of mercy to rescue me and Sheila.'

'No drinking on duty!' snapped Daviot.

'But I insist,' said Peter. 'One glass won't put anyone over the limit.'

'Oh, very well,' conceded Daviot.

Hamish groaned inwardly. He always got the better of Blair because Blair was stupid. But this Fox was a new danger. The trouble was that Daviot needed someone to crawl to him and praise him on a daily basis, and Blair filled that role.

He also saw Jimmy reaching eagerly for a glass. Hamish remembered a former Benedictine monk he had met when the man was on a walking tour. He had found him downing whiskies with the locals at the bar on the waterfront and entertaining everyone with tales of the monastery. Hamish now remembered him saying with a gentle smile, 'The Holy Roman Church is right down on sex, but they are simply marvellous when it comes to booze. We all used to look forward to a visit from the bishop. How the wine would flow!' It seemed now as if this rather strict Scottish church saw nothing wrong with the stuff, either.

He found Daviot approaching him. 'Where is Carter?' he demanded.

'As my suspicions could have turned out to be nothing more than a flight of fancy, I had to leave him to handle things back in Lochdubh. The colonel is right pleased with him,' Hamish went on, with that vague look in his hazel eyes which meant he was lying, 'because Carter evicted two bad troublemakers from the bar. And, sir, when the colonel praised him, Charlie said it was because of your training, sir.'

Daviot beamed. 'Splendid, splendid.'

And I'm as bad a creep as the rest of them, thought Hamish as Daviot walked away.

They finally got the news that the crime scene was free for examination. Blair said that Hamish should go and type up his report at police headquarters and that he and his detectives could do the rest.

Glad to escape, Hamish drove to Strathbane. He had two thermoses he always carried with him and had them filled up at one of the new coffee shops in Strathbane. He found a spare computer in the detectives' room and

221

began to type, but always aware that somewhere below his feet in the cells was Harriet Munro. He had liked her. If he hadn't been so busy playing Pygmalion, his wits might have been sharper and he might have recognized the danger.

On and on he typed, half his mind wondering how Blair would cope with the new threat of Fox.

Fox managed to see that Blair was supplied with more whisky. He did not realize that although Blair was relatively stupid when it came to detection, he was as sharp as a tack concerning his own self-preservation, and so Fox did not notice that most of Blair's whisky was ending up in the font, unnoticed until the following Sunday when the about-to-be-christened baby was saved at the last minute from having a face splashed with water and alcohol.

And Blair knew exactly why Fox was plying him with drink and a deep, red hatred blossomed inside his fat hairy bosom.

In the scramble to get to the crime scene, Blair had taken his own car, a small Peugeot. He knew that the air bag on his side worked but not on the passenger side, a fact he had discovered when he had run into a fire hydrant, his wife beside him; his wife only survived because it was a twenty-mile-an-hour zone.

'How did you get here?' Blair asked Fox.

'With Jimmy Anderson.'

'Why don't we leave them to it, laddie,' said Blair,

with a fat smile. 'She didnae kill anyone here in the kirk, jist tied 'em up.'

Fox agreed. Daviot had left, so there was no point in hanging around to impress anyone.

Blair drove steadily along the heathery one-track roads. He was very tired and his eyes were gritty with lack of sleep. A red sun was staring right in his eyes and he mumbled and pulled the sun visor down. He glanced sideways. Young Fox was asleep.

As he finally crested the top of the hill that led down into Strathbane, he could see one of the rare trees of Sutherland halfway along. He put his foot down and the little car surged forward. He hit the tree at sixty miles per hour. His air bag exploded against his body, but Fox, without one, was thrown violently against the windscreen, shattered the glass, and lay half in, half out of the car.

When Blair struggled out, he found himself horrified at what he had done. Fox's face was bluish white, the bits of it that could be seen through a mask of red blood. Dizzy and frightened, Blair stumbled along to the nearest croft house which was well off the road and up on the moors. He rang the bell and fell unconscious on the doorstep.

Fox was not dead. He slowly recovered consciousness. Rain was beginning to fall, cool rain washing the blood from his face. He dragged himself back into the car, letting out yelps of pain, sure he had broken his ribs.

He eased into the driver's seat behind the deflated air bag and started the engine. Only later did he realize how lucky he had been that the car had not burst into flames. He reversed the car, which gave a howling grinding noise as the front bumper, caught on a low tree branch, was torn off. Half stunned and barely aware of what he was doing, he drove at thirty miles an hour to Strathbane Hospital.

An ambulance, a fire engine, and a police car arrived at the croft to find a recovered Blair being administered to by the crofter's wife. The paramedics said he should allow himself to be taken to hospital for checks. In his initial statement, Blair said he had been driven off the road by a gang of bikers. Poor Henry Fox, mourned Blair.

Other police returned and said there was no sign of the car. Blair turned white and nearly fainted.

Hamish had just finished his report when he heard the news of Fox's 'accident'. He decided to visit the hospital and see him after he had delivered all the copies of his report.

He bought a bunch of grapes from the hospital shop and, following directions, found young Fox in a private room.

Fox was conscious. When he saw Hamish, he said, 'Where is Detective Chief Inspector Blair?'

'Somewhere in this hospital, I think,' said Hamish. 'What happened?'

'I don't know. I was asleep.'

'I heard you didn't have an air bag.'

'Bad luck that,' said Fox. 'I wonder if Blair knew that.'

'Possibly,' said Hamish.

'Do you mean, he tried to murder me!'

'I'm sure he didn't,' lied Hamish. 'But hear this. Blair is arch-toady around here. Two of you competing to see who could be the biggest would make you look a fool and damage any hope of promotion.'

'And end up like you? Stuck up in the back of beyond?'

'But alive,' said Hamish. 'Watch your back.'

As Hamish drove back to Lochdubh, he felt a shiver go down his spine as he thought of Blair. The whisky must finally have begun to get to the detective's brain. He had just shown himself capable of murder. And it wasn't only young Fox who should look out!

Epilogue

See the happy moron,
He doesn't give a damn,
I wish I were a moron,
My God! I think I am!
—Anonymous

A week later, Hamish got a visit from Jimmy Anderson. To Hamish's relief, Jimmy showed no signs of wanting alcohol, settling happily for a cup of strong coffee. Hamish put out deck chairs in the front garden because it was a fine sunny day with only the faintest of breezes rustling through the rambling roses that hung over the blue police lamp.

'Have some shortbread,' said Hamish. 'It's from the minister's wife as a peace offering. She tried to tie me up with her niece and has only just found out that said niece is as daft as a brush when it comes to men and thinks she's Cleopatra.'

'Thanks, I will,' said Jimmy, reaching down and taking a piece of shortbread from a plate on the grass between the chairs. 'Did I tell ye? I've been invited to Dick and Anka's wedding?'

'No, you didn't. I still wonder why she chose Dick?'

'It's like this,' said Jimmy. 'It's like, say, a top violinist with a Strad meets another with a Strad and they're both the best.'

'Don't get it.'

'Baps are like music. They should write an anthem to the Scottish bap. Dick always was obsessed with cakes and along comes the cake and bap-maker supreme.'

'So sex disnae come into it?' asked Hamish, scratching his fiery head.

'Cakes *are* sexy. I bet there are American cops who would kill for a decent cream doughnut.'

'Oh, well. I'll never understand. How's Harriet bearing up?'

'Quiet. Reads a lot.'

'Put a suicide watch on her.'

'Why?'

'Right down in there afore she got twisted is a warm-hearted clever woman. She won't be able to live with herself for much longer. I know she's basically good.'

'Hamish, you cannae go around bumping off people and be basically good.'

'I don't know.' Hamish scratched Lugs's ears and gave Sally a bit of shortbread. 'I think we're all capable of murder if someone treats us so badly that our brains get damaged. And talking of damaged brains, what about Blair and Fox?'

227

'Oh, Blair was probably drunk or sleepy. The bikers he claims forced him off the road are nowhere to be found.'

'He knew the air bag on the passenger side didn't work because his wife told me,' said Hamish. 'I'm telling you: He tried to kill Fox.'

'Havers, Hamish. He's an old swine. But kill anyone! Naw.'

But Hamish felt uneasily that Blair had finally crossed some sort of line. He privately resolved to have a quiet word with Fox.

But the days were lazy and fine, and Hamish had almost forgotten his decision to warn Fox. That was until the man himself appeared one day at the police station just as Hamish was finishing his breakfast.

'What brings you?' asked Hamish. 'Coffee?'

'I am curious about you,' said Fox. 'I came to see why a bright copper like you would want to stay stuck up here. I took a look around and I still can't figure it out.'

'Sit down. Have a coffee. Help yourself to milk and sugar. The trouble is you are ower-ambitious and it makes you blind to everything else. You do realize that Blair made an attempt to kill you?'

Fox had just helped himself to a mug of coffee and he had been about to add milk. He held the jug frozen in the air. Then he slowly poured a little milk and set the jug back down on the table.

'The bikers,' he said.

'I dinnae believe for a moment that there were any bikers,' said Hamish. 'Blair knew the air bag on the passenger side didnae work because he and his wife were in an accident not so long ago. He fears you'll take his job because you're a better creep than he is.'

Fox looked amused at the insult. 'Is there any other way to get on in the force?'

Hamish sighed. 'There was a time, or so the old retired coppers have told me, when they went into the job to help the community. Yes, they could be rough and tough, but there was a streak of altruism in them just the same. I think Blair has crossed some sort of line.'

Fox laughed. 'Unless I get to him first.'

Hamish felt a jolt of alarm. He hadn't really meant that. Or had he?

He stood up. 'I have chores to do. Why not take a look around? Lochdubh is beautiful.'

'Okay. Thanks for the coffee.'

Strolling along the waterfront, faced by some of the most beautiful scenery in the Highlands, all Fox saw was a dead-end sort of backwater. That was until he saw a vision strolling along the waterfront, sunlight shining in her blonde hair. He rushed up. 'May I help you?'

She looked amused. 'As you are obviously a stranger here, it is probably I who can help you.'

He stuck out his hand. 'Detective Constable Henry Fox at your service, ma'am.'

'Priscilla Halburton-Smythe at yours. Now I must get on. I am going to see Hamish.'

She had her back to the police station as she was talking to him and over her shoulder, Fox saw Hamish send one hunted look down the waterfront and then disappear.

He said goodbye and waited, leaning on the sun-warmed wall of the waterfront. She came back slowly.

'Not there?' he asked. 'Never mind. What about a drink.'

'Too early,' said Priscilla and walked quickly away to where her car was parked.

That was class, thought Fox. With high rank and pay, he could get himself one of those. And yet, what had such a gorgeous creature been doing wasting her time on Hamish?

Hamish's sudden realization that he was to be best man at Dick's wedding hit him when he got an anguished call from Anka, summoning him to the wedding rehearsal. In all the subsequent fuss, in all the heady emotion of seeing Dick and Anka married, in all the subsequent pain of a momentous hangover, Hamish forgot all about Fox.

As stocky little Dick walked down the aisle with the glorious auburn-haired vision that was Anka in white lace, Hamish, like every man in the church, wondered for the hundredth time how it was that Dick of all people had snared such a bride. Then there was the

230

reception at a large marquee just outside the village. The Polish relatives had arrived with a crate of 150-proof Polish vodka, and the Currie sisters and Mrs Wellington fell over during an impromptu show of tai chi.

But Fox had not forgotten Blair. He discovered, to his chagrin, that on Daviot's wedding anniversary Blair was invited to the small and exclusive dinner party along with the procurator fiscal and the lord-lieutenant of Sutherland.

Like all Celts, he was passionate and capable of fierce hatreds and resentments. He had been watching a number of real-life crime stories on television, mostly American ones, and was fascinated, as Hamish had been, at how many cases of poisoning had gone undetected. Blair smoked heavily. Fox had read about a case recently where a child had died after drinking the contents of a refill for an e-cigarette. Put three of them in a bottle of liqueur, say, ran his thoughts, and send it anonymously to Blair as a present. At first, he dismissed his idea as pure fantasy, but then it would not go away, until one day he drove as far as Wick and bought a bottle of Drambuie and three refill bottles – 'the strongest for my e-cigarette' – in a tiny Asian supermarket where they did not appear to have CCTV. For every three people in the British Isles, there is one CCTV camera, so he felt triumphant at actually having tracked down a place without one.

Back in Strathbane, he wrapped the bottle up in fancy paper, blessing the Asians who could cram so many things into one small shop. He found out Blair's address and on his day off, waited outside in a hired car. He saw Blair leave for work. Still, he waited. Then Blair's wife, Mary, came down the steps and got into a car and drove off. It was then Fox realized that there was probably some damn camera somewhere in the street.

He drove off, went home, and found a cardboard box. He set out again for that store in Wick, where he bought bubble wrap and duct tape. In his excitement, he forgot to wear gloves. He packed up the bottle and addressed it to Blair. The shop was also a sub-post-office, but he did not want to be remembered and if he posted it there, it could be tracked. He retreated all the way back down to Strathbane, put on a disguise, and posted it from the main post office.

Mary, Blair's wife, although an ex-prostitute, was an exemplary wife and adored by Mrs Daviot because clever Mary had quickly transformed herself into a woman who wore well-cut tweeds and spoke with a posh accent. But underneath, the old Mary was always there: tough, clever, and ruthless. Blair suited her very well and her past career had taught her how to manage drunks.

When the box with the Drambuie arrived, she slowly drew it out. There was no card. She packed it up again and went to the local pharmacy and asked the

232

pharmacist if he would make sure there was nothing odd in it. She didn't bother to tell Blair about it because he came home, as usual, late and drunk.

A week later, she was startled when the pharmacist phoned her to say that there was enough nicotine in the Drambuie to kill any man who was a smoker and not in perfect health. So a police investigation was started. The news buzzed round headquarters and Fox was stricken with fear. He thought he must have run mad.

He had heard what happened to policemen in prison. It would possibly be shown on the television programme *Crime Scotland*, and the bottle would be held up. That shopkeeper might recognize it. Something on his day off impelled him towards Lochdubh.

It was a misty day with the sun just beginning to break through, turning the loch to a sheet of gold. There was the smell of frying bacon coming from the police station as Fox knocked nervously at the door. The door opened and the tall figure of Hamish Macbeth looked down at him.

'Come in,' ordered Hamish. 'Sit down, drink coffee, and tell me why on earth you tried to murder Mr Blair.'

'You can't possibly know,' wailed Fox. 'Who saw me?'

'No one. Look, Blair tried to kill you, so you try to kill Blair. He got away with it and you won't. Right?'

'Right,' said Fox. 'My fingerprints are on that bottle. All our fingerprints at headquarters are on file.' And, having said that, he burst into tears.

'Sit down! That's better.' Hamish tore off a sheet of kitchen paper. 'Dry your eyes. Put a good lot of sugar in that coffee. First, you'll need to leave the police force. You're not cut out for it. Now tell me where you bought the stuff.'

Fox described his trip to Wick and to the Asian shopkeeper. When he had finished, Hamish said, 'We must get the evidence. If I didnae hae a good understanding of how Blair can drive a man to murder, I wouldnae be helping ye.

'I assume thon bottle is in forensics.'

Fox nodded.

'You may be in luck. There is a shinty match tonight over in Golspie. I overheard someone saying the forensic boys were all going. So we get over there, break in, take an innocent bottle, substitute it, and that should do the trick.'

A little colour returned to Fox's pale cheeks. 'Can you do it?'

'Can we do it, you mean,' said Hamish. 'Now, I don't suppose you've eaten anything, so I'll make you a bacon bap. I'm going fishing on the loch so you can come with me. Tell me again where you bought the stuff.'

Fox enjoyed that day on the loch almost wistfully, the way people look back on and wish for the innocence of childhood.

Soon it was evening and unfortunately it was light all night long. Fox could not guess how on earth Hamish expected to break in. He knew the place was heavily burglar-alarmed.